Spotter

Billy Morris

ISBN: 9798317333096

Print Edition

Copyright 2025 Billy Morris

All Rights reserved. No part of this book may be reproduced in any form without the prior permission of the author.

Spotter is a work of fiction. All characters are wholly fictitious. Any similarity to real persons, living or dead, is entirely coincidental and not intended by the author. All situations, locations, opinions, history and dialogues are in no way intended to depict or reflect actual events or facts.

The author can be contacted at
BM.Author@outlook.com

Billy Morris was born in Leeds, Yorkshire in 1966. He left Leeds in the late 1990's and has lived and worked in Europe and USA. He now lives mainly in South-East Asia.

He wrote his first book 'Bournemouth 90' in 2021, the sequel 'LS92' was published in 2022.

His third book 'Birdsong on Holbeck Moor' was published in October 2022.

The final books in the Eighties Leeds series, LS65 and Paris 75 were published in 2023 and 2024.

Accents, Dialects and Pronunciation

Spotter is set in Leeds, a city in West Yorkshire in the North of England. The Leeds accent could generally be described as 'Yorkshire' but is quite distinct, and is easily identifiable when compared to speech in other parts of the county. Even different areas of the city have their own distinct dialects.

People in Leeds tend to miss out letters, join words together and speak quite quickly. It's not an exaggeration to say that a conversation between Leeds folk could sound like a foreign language when compared to 'BBC English.'

Including dialogue exactly as it would most likely be spoken, would therefore make this book unreadable for many people. However, there are certain fundamental elements of the Leeds accent which I felt needed to be reflected, in order to maintain a level of authenticity in the characters' speech. The following substitutions have therefore been made throughout the book- -

The most obvious is the dropping of the word 'the' before a noun. In Leeds 'the' will be replaced by what linguists call a glottal stop. Execution of this element of the Leeds accent is generally difficult for a non-Yorkshire native. Actors on TV and in films usually get it wrong by either missing out 'the' entirely, or pronouncing a 't' in its place. As a Leeds speaker, I can't even explain how to execute a glottal stop. Google tells me it's achieved by rapidly closing the vocal chords. I've no idea how you do that. If you want to hear an example, I suggest you listen to an interview with David Batty or Kalvin Phillips. They're both experts. In the book, a glottal stop to replace 'the' is denoted by an apostrophe (').

"We're going to the pub' would therefore become "We're off to 'pub".

Owt, Nowt and Summat – The words anything, nothing and something will usually be replaced by owt, nowt and summat by a native Leeds speaker. The pronunciation of these words is open to some debate, but based on my own experience, I would say that owt is pronounced 'oat' and nowt is pronounced 'note', although I am aware that in some outlying parts of the city, both words would rhyme with 'shout'. Summat is universally pronounced 'summert'.

I recognise it may be confusing to include speech patterns which are unrecognisable beyond the boundaries of West Yorkshire, but I felt that dialect would become unrealistic in the context of the story without at least including these substitutions. I hope this doesn't impact on your enjoyment of the book.

Chapter 1

The room is warm and dry and my eyelids feel heavy, my mouth dry, the metallic taste of last night's Caffrey's still tainting my tongue. I blink my eyes wide and focus on Chief Inspector Tony Hudson's mouth. His teeth. Too small, like a child's, a jagged line of beige porcelain, evenly separated by a three millimetre gap. I stare at the teeth until he closes his mouth and licks his lips and sniffs, then turns to the man sitting next to him.

"Are we ready Ken?"

Chief Inspector Kenneth Baxter flares his nostrils and grunts his agreement, and Hudson picks up his pen and taps a pad on the desk in front of him, then looks to my left, from where I can smell the harsh citrus perfume of Cathy King, my Police Federation Rep. The smell almost makes me retch.

"Okay, so...thanks all for coming here to Wakefield today, hopefully the trip over the '62 wasn't too arduous Ken?"

Kenneth Baxter twitches his nose and raises his eyebrows and grunts again.

"And PC Mills, obviously just back from duty in Spain." He looks at me in a way that suggests he can tell I haven't slept in two days, so I stay silent.

"So, given that this is a joint West Yorkshire - Greater Manchester...erm...enquiry, we felt it appropriate to have the meeting on neutral ground as it were."

Hudson smiles and nods at his own joke, as I shuffle in my seat to disguise an ominous rumble coming from deep in my stomach.

"Shall I start Ken? Maybe as I was Silver Commander on the day in question?"

Baxter flicks the fingers of his right hand dismissively as my blurred gaze moves from Hudson's eyes back to his teeth.

"So, PC Mills...we're here today for a preliminary, fact-finding meeting to discuss the events of 3rd March 2001. This is not a formal investigation as of yet, at this stage it's an opportunity for yourself and PC Molloy to state the facts of what occurred from your point of view. Would you agree that's what we're here for today Ken?"

Ken Baxter slowly lifts his eyes from his pad and sighs deeply and rubs at a rogue patch of stubble on his sweaty red chin as he looks down his nose at me.

"Okay...PC Mills...3rd March."

I sniff and swallow the globule of mucous that has lodged itself in my throat and croak a response.

"That was Man United at home."

"Yes, the Leeds -Manchester United Premier league football game. For clarity..." Tony Hudson shifts his focus to Cathy King and flashes his primary school smile. "On the day, I was Silver Commander and PC Mills was the FIO, the football intelligence officer responsible for Leeds United games. PC Lee Molloy was the GMP FIO attached to Manchester United."

Hudson turns back towards me and the smile vanishes.

"Where do you want me to start?"

I direct the question towards Hudson, but the answer comes loudly and suddenly from Ken Baxter.

"How about the previous Wednesday?"

I cough as I feel the gob of mucous make a reappearance in my throat. I sense Cathy King shuffle in her seat next to me, but don't want to risk looking in her direction. There is an awkward silence, which Tony Hudson breaks.

"The previous Wednesday Ken? The final pre-match planning meet-up, yes?"

Ken Baxter tilts his head back and raises his eyebrows, as he regards me with suspicion, leaving me in no doubt that he expects me to respond.

"Yes, Lee...PC Molloy and I met that day to finalise plans for the match which, obviously was a Category..."

Before I've finished my sentence, Baxter intervenes.

"And where did that meeting take place?"

"Initially at Holbeck police station..." I'm facing Hudson but can see Baxter smirking and nodding beside him. "...but then we reconvened to the Waggon and Horses public house."

"Planning meetings in the pub hey? Pub lunch and a couple of pints was it?" Baxter chuckles to himself and his red face turns purple.

"No sir, the Waggon isn't really the sort of pub where you'd have lunch. It's popular with Leeds supporters, we called in to see the landlady."

"And was there specific intelligence at that point, of the area around the pub being a potential flashpoint?" Tony Hudson scribbles on his pad without looking up.

"Nothing definite sir, but one of my intelligence sources had said that word on the street was that a couple of characters with Manchester accents had been drinking in the Waggon..."

"Characters with Manchester accents?" Ken Baxter is shaking with laughter now. "Who are we talking about, Bernard Manning and those dickheads from The Oasis?"

"That's what I'd heard sir." My mouth is dry and I glance towards the plastic cup of water on the desk but my hands are shaking so much I have to push them beneath my legs to keep them still.

"Wire cutters." Baxter pushes out his bottom lip and folds his arms and looks down his nose at me. I glance towards Cathy King who looks nervously back at me then at Baxter, and I get the feeling she's out of her depth.

"Wire cutters Ken?" Tony Hudson shakes his head then looks at me and shrugs. I shake my head too and the movement makes my vision blur.

"Okay!" Ken Baxter slams the palms of both hands down on the desk, causing Cathy and Tony Hudson to jump. "Let's stop dancing round our handbags. I assume we all know the reason why we're here. If not, I'll state the facts. One of the targets arrested in the dawn raids by GMP following the disorder in Holbeck in March, has made some serious allegations. His solicitor is now threatening to make those allegations public, should his client's case go to trial. We need to establish whether there is any substance to those allegations before formulating our response." Baxter removes his hands from the table and sits back in his chair and straightens his tie.

"PC Mills..."

"Yes sir." I can feel a dewdrop of snot attempting to exit my left nostril and sniff hard, then worry it might sound like I'm crying.

"After visiting the Waggon and Horses, where did you and PC Molloy go?"

"Back to the car sir."

"Straight back to the car?" Tony Hudson chips in, obviously eager to remain in the conversation.

"Yes...well, no actually sir, we stopped and spoke to one of the girls who was smoking outside the...erm, sauna next to the Waggon. It had been snowing and she was only wearing a..."

"Did you go to the footbridge?" Baxter's booming tone is now just short of what could be termed a shout.

"Footbridge? No sir." I shiver involuntarily as I recall an icy March wind chasing the '621 off the Pennines, howling across the bridge with the ghosts of old Holbeck, the brickworks, Islington cricket ground and the New Peacock, all lost to the seventies motorway.

Baxter slowly picks up a pair of glasses from the desk, turns a page in his pad and runs his finger along the line.

"Tilbury Row? Did the two of you visit Tilbury Row that afternoon?"

I shake my head and shrug again, but Ken Baxter isn't looking.

"Did you climb the grass banking and access an area bordering Matthew Murray school playing field?"

I glance at Cathy King chewing the top of her pen, and recall slush and mud and motorway rubbish hanging like bad fruit in bare trees.

"Did you locate an area of broken fencing alongside the A643 roundabout, which PC Molloy opened up using a pair of wire cutters?"

I expect Cathy King to stand and shout 'objection' but she just flinches and clicks her pen on her teeth.

Ken Baxter exhales loudly and puffs out his cheeks and Tony Hudson sighs and a silence descends on the room.

"Can I just verify how reliable a source the complainant is? I mean presumably he's just using this as a means to get the charges dropped?" Cathy has removed the pen from her mouth and is jabbing it back and forth in front of her nose.

"Of course he is. I know that, you know that, and his brief knows it. He's also saying that Molloy told the risk group of Man United fans to hold back and avoid the buses back to the station after the game. He says Molloy gave them directions to the gap in the fence and where to go when they reached the other side. He's not the main problem though." Baxter turns to Tony Hudson who pauses and considers his own pad.

"Erm...yes, we also have three statements from our own team on the day." Hudson screws up his face and I feel my bowels churn. "Evidence Gathering Team member 'C' says that outside the stadium after the match he saw PC Molloy 'apparently directing the Manchester Risk supporters towards the Elland Road roundabout.' He claims that as they followed the group, Molloy shared the information relating to the wire cutters and the fence."

The room falls silent again. Cathy taps her pen on her teeth, Baxter rocks in his seat and stares at the desk and Tony Hudson licks at his lips and blinks quickly. I clench my buttocks to retain control of my bowels, and the Caffrey's tainting my tongue starts to taste like sour milk.

Baxter sighs loudly and reaches across and taps Hudson's pad.

"Yes, unfortunately, there's more, and this pertains to you PC Mills." He doesn't look at me as he speaks.

"EGT team member 'E' reports that whilst a significant disturbance was occurring at the Waggon and Horses public house, with Leeds supporters being prevented from leaving the pub by officers, he was instructed to remain on the footbridge by PC Mills, who told him to focus his longest lens on the bottom of Tilbury Mount. This was six minutes before the Manchester supporters appeared on Ingram Road and engaged in violence with Leeds supporters. In the words of EGT team member 'E', he was perfectly positioned on the footbridge to capture images of the ensuing violence. Almost too perfectly positioned for it to be chance."

"It's almost as if someone had a premonition of where the fighting would occur Tony." Ken Baxter seems to be struggling to suppress a smirk.

Tony Hudson doesn't look up and continues to read from his pad, his next sentence preceded by a sharp intake of breath.

"The next statement comes from one of our own matchday team, who we'll refer to as Officer Y."

Officer Y. How fucking imaginative. Eddie Bastard Young.

"Officer Y says that when the Manchester supporters appeared on Tilbury Row and engaged a smaller group of Leeds supporters, PC Mills was seen making a mobile phone call and was heard to say, and I quote. 'They're here now. Get everyone out of the pub. I don't fucking care. Just do it.'"

"Bullshit." This time I'm talking before he's finished. "Apologies sir, but that's nonsense. I don't recognise that account at all."

"Why would three separate colleagues concoct those statements if they're untrue?" Ken Baxter's pen is poised above his pad as if he wants me to come up with something half plausible, but Cathy King gets there first.

"Can I clarify Chief Inspector, that the statements from matchday colleagues were only made after the solicitor lodged his complaint?"

Baxter nods.

"And EGT and matchday support officers with extensive football experience would be obvious candidates for any future FIO vacancy? A role with a top Premier League club, presenting the opportunity of travel to destinations around the UK and Europe?"

Baxter and Hudson both remain silent, but the point clearly lands as Cathy drives home the point.

"So, everyone who has made these allegations has some skin in the game...they all stand to gain if PCs Mills and Molloy are sanctioned over this incident. An incident, which, let us not forget, has resulted in an extensive intelligence operation which led to the arrest of a number of Category C hooligans."

The Chief Inspectors have stopped writing and are almost nodding as she finishes speaking, and I keep my mouth tightly shut to avoid lapsing into any semblance of a smile.

"Okay PC Mills, Cathy, I think we'll leave it there for now. Thanks for coming Cathy." Hudson and Baxter remain seated as Cathy and I stand and head to the door. Cathy holds the door open and I'm almost away when I hear Hudson's voice.

"PC Mills?"

I turn to face the thin white lips and the tiny teeth again.

"You're heading to London now?"

"Yes sir, West Ham tomorrow."

He nods. "Good. I need to see you in my office on Monday. 9am. Don't be late."

Cathy King leads the way from the meeting room, and is greeted by the leering grin of Lee Molloy, sat alongside his Fed Rep and nodding appreciatively at her above-the-knee skirt and zip-sided boots.

"Now then pal, good trip to Coruna? How'd it go with the gaffers in there?" Lee stands, smiling and extends his hand. He's wearing a bright yellow Stone Island anorak, blue Paul & Shark cap and white Stan Smiths.

"Alright, I think..." I glance over as Cathy and her colleague confer quietly out of earshot. "Nice to see you made the effort with your uniform..."

"Derby day tomorrow pal. Straight out round town this afternoon but these cunts still dragged me over here for this. Fuck em. What happened then?"

"Nowt. Kept my mouth shut. Couple of EGT and one of ours have given statements though."

"Fuckers...know who it is?" Lee leans in too close and the smell of old tobacco turns my stomach.

"I'm guessing that wanker Eddie Young. Heard me on the phone to Shivers."

"What did you say then?"

"Denied it all. Said it never happened. They didn't push it."

Lee Molloy smiles and grips my left arm with his right hand as his union rep stands and nods his head towards the meeting room door.

"I fucking told you. This investigation is going to collapse like Bowyer and Woodgate's trial mate, it's going nowhere. They're just going through the motions so they can say they've looked into it. They don't care. They got dawn raids, press coverage and convictions. They're happy."

"And you got the lads you needed out of the way."

"We're home and dry mate, trust me." Lee Molloy winks and slaps me on the arm. "And have a good weekend in the big smoke pal, hope the ICF don't turn your boys over!"

Chapter 2

"No charge mate, assuming you're here on business?" The forty-something bloke on the left-luggage counter at Kings Cross nods towards my WYP cap badge as I hand over my rucksack. He stinks of weed and I wonder if I should tell him, but I guess he probably knows, so I take the ticket and head out into the early Saturday morning hustle of the station.

I glance at my watch. 7.10. The first train doesn't get in for half an hour and the bookies isn't open, so I decide to wander round to the Duke of York. The taste of last night's Guinness is souring my breath and demanding some food or a cigarette. Not a hard decision, but I can't risk a smoke in uniform, so I duck into the porn mag shop on York Way and spark up a Marlboro Light. The fat bloke behind the counter cranes his neck around a rack of dildos to see what I'm doing, so I pick up a DVD called 'Anal Gapers 4' and wave it at him and smile so he knows he isn't about to be raided.

I suck on the cig and check my Nokia 3310. No word from the lads, or my colleagues. I rummage in my trouser pocket and pull out a scrap of lined paper bearing a biro scrawl reading 'Beehive Inn, London, N15. 1 x single room, 1 meal, 1 breakfast. £75 paid cash.' I carefully place the slip of paper in my wallet and smile to myself at a good tip from Lee Molloy. Drink as much as you want, plus a cardboard burger and a single bed in a room smaller than the average cell. All for fifty quid. The clever part is they give you a receipt for £75, so you get a free night out and make £25 on it off your expenses claim. Out of the way too, just off Tottenham High Road. Well away from Camden, Kings Cross, Covent Garden or anywhere else Leeds fans are likely to turn up. Not that there was much chance of that last night. Leeds' European adventures are stretching most lads' resources to the limit, and a lot aren't even bothering today.

The fat man behind the counter coughs loudly, and I read the sleeve notes of 'Revenge of the Czech Piss Slaves' as I finish my cig. I'm about to ask if has the first in the series when the Nokia pings in my pocket, so I hold up the illuminated green screen to show him and head to the door.

'Quiet on train. Few got on at Donny. ETA 7.45. Meet at ticket barrier?' A text from Eddie Young. Him and the evidence gathering photographer are already on the job. I turn right and walk to the Duke of York on the corner. A couple of lads I don't know are pacing outside, smoking and jabbing fingers at their phone keypads.

"Alright lads. Come down last night?"

"Flew back into Gatwick. Thought there was no point going up and back so we stayed down here."

"You must be loaded."

"Fuck that. This European run is ruining me mate. I'm going to be divorced by 'end of 'season."

I smile and push open the door. The Duke of York's status as a residential hotel allows it to serve alcohol to guests to accompany a meal, 24 hours a day. How that translates to 150 lads drinking and sharing five bowls of peanuts and four bedrooms is never quite explained. Not today though. Only a dozen heads turn towards me as I enter the bar. Mostly drinkers and out-of-town Leeds fans, no one of much interest. I nod greetings and get the usual muttered replies. A couple of Strongbow shirt-wearers are propping up the bar and turn their heads as I approach.

"What do you think today then lads? Smith's suspended isn't he?"

"Yeah, Keane will be alright though. Unbeaten in eleven. I think we'll do 'em."

"Rio's first game back there too. He'll get some stick."

"We'll be right. 3-1, Leeds. Get your money on that."

I smile. My reputation clearly goes before me, and I've already got twenty on 2-1.

I exit the pub and head down York Way and into the station. At the barrier I spot Eddie Young before he sees me, striding down the platform, a helmet taller than anyone else, smug-twat-smirk and thumbs tucked into his Hi-Vis at chest level. A young EGT photographer is struggling to keep up with him, lugging a heavy bag of kit, but Young doesn't look back, he scans the barrier until he spots me, then lifts his chin in acknowledgement without smiling.

"Millsy." Eddie Young flashes his warrant card at the ticket collector and pushes his way past as Pierre, the EGT kid, struggles through the barrier.

"You alright there mate? Need a hand?"

He looks embarrassed and smiles, and I wonder if he's one of the wankers who grassed me up about Man.U.

"What's the plan then?" Eddie Young looks beyond me, monitoring a group of lads who are acting shifty at the barrier, trying to get two through on one ticket.

"I've already had a look in the Duke of York. Scotsman isn't open yet. Our main lads aren't getting in till 9.30. Might as well head straight up to Forest Gate. Briefing is at 9."

Eddie Young nods and sniffs.

"How was Spain? Owt happen?" He was meant to be on the trip but got bumped to let a sergeant go to 'get some experience.' Truth is it was the usual shit and hassle of dealing with foreign police who don't want you on their patch, and Leeds fans who are so pissed they don't know if they're in Malaga or Miggy. I'm not telling him that though.

"Fucking brilliant mate. Great trip, lovely city, weather was great and we got the result. Shame you had to miss out. Hope same doesn't happen for the semi eh?" I exchange a glance with Pierre and give him a wink.

Young doesn't bite and changes the subject. "What happened last night? Did you meet up with West Ham's spotter?"

"Erm, no, I got a whisper that some of our banned lot were down last night and boozing in Camden. I went up there."

"Didn't the West Ham bloke want to go with you? He's a bit keen from what I've heard."

"No, he wasn't...erm, I thought it best I went on my own, didn't want to go in mob handed, you know."

There's a slight smirk on Eddie Young's face, and I see him shaking his head out of the corner of my eye as we go down the steps into the underground, him calling over his shoulder that East Ham is the nearest station to the nick, with me and EGT Pierre trailing behind like kids on a school trip.

I swerve them on the train, hanging back to stand by the door as they sit down, and I look down the half full carriage as Young bores Pierre with his matchday war stories. My mouth feels dry and I shuffle under the weight of my kit, leaning back against the door to stop a rivulet of sweat making its way down my spine. At Bow

Road, a disembodied, half-chant echoes along the platform and Young is up, head out of the door, alert and itching for action. I catch EGT Pierre's eye again and smile and shake my head.

At the reception desk at Forest Gate, Eddie Young strides forward and announces our presence. 'West Yorkshire Football Liaison team.' The Asian WPC in the hijab smiles and points to some seats by the door and I sit, trying not to remember the last time I was here. Blood on the tiles, a woman screaming, Met stab vests, Glocks and baseball caps, hand on my shoulder, get the fuck out, back door job. A lifetime ago.

"PC Mills?" The silver crew-cut of Vic Bright, West Ham's legendary FIO appears round a heavy blue door and I stand and extend my hand.

"This is PC Eddie Young and Pierre Bernard, EGT support." I gesture over my shoulder and Vic Bright leads us through the doors and up the stairs, to a meeting room bursting with black jackets and Hi-Vis, smelling of sweat and tobacco and machine coffee.

"Grab a cuppa lads, my gaffer will be on in a minute." Bright scans the room, waving and winking greetings.

"Who is Silver Commander today?" Youngy is eager to know whose arse he'll be licking.

"Inspector Bowen. He's alright. Does it by the book. Plays the game. You know the sort..."

I know the sort alright and I'm already planning my exit when he strides into the room, prompting a flurry of seat scraping as the assembled ranks find somewhere to sit. I position myself in a seat behind a tall copper with a shaved head, and my eyelids are already starting to feel heavy as he launches into the usual pre-match bollocks of POPS command structures, rapid response EGT's and

Stadium Safety Advisory Group adherence. I give it five minutes then slide the phone out of my pocket, flick into the messages and press send.

I'm already out of my seat when the chirp of the Nokia ring tone interrupts Inspector Bowen and he glares as I push my way along the row, flashing the screen at Vic Bright as I pass.

"My contact with our main lads." I whisper as I pass and head to the door.

"Now then...Hello.. Are you there?" The line crackles then drops out. I flick into the 'calls' menu and select 'Shivers', then redial.

"Hello...Millsy? Can you hear me?"

"I can now yeah. Where are you?" I press the phone to my ear, hearing car horns louder than his voice.

"Just landed at Kings Cross."

"How many?"

"Hundred or so, most of them have gone to 'Duke of York. We're on our way down to 'Mabel Tavern, out of 'way."

I pause, knowing what that means - the presence of banned Cat C lads who have an exclusion zone around stadiums and stations, and the potential to meet up with a similar group from another club. I mentally assess the other London fixtures.

"Forest?"

"Yeah, it's one of their lads' 30th apparently. They're bringing a good mob down. Most aren't going to be arsed going right down to Wimbledon."

"Right, you're going to the game though?"

The sound down the line becomes more muffled. and I can tell they've reached the pub.

"Yeah, we'll have a couple here then head up to Liverpool Street. Have you got the addresses?"

"Have you got my money?" I lower my voice and glance over my shoulder as two motorbike officers climb the stairs, removing their helmets.

"Don't worry Millsy, you'll get your cash. Hamilton Hall at twelve. Text when you get there and I'll see you in the bogs. Don't fucking talk to me in front of anyone."

The line goes dead and I walk back to the briefing room and peer through the glass in the door. Inspector Bowen is still talking about dispersal tactics and risk profiling, so I head back down the stairs and into the car park. I duck down behind a TSG van and spark up a Marlboro, squatting between the parked cars while chugging on the cig and looking up at a CCTV camera revolving on a post above me.

I calculate that two cigs should be about right and time it perfectly, removing my phone from my ear as I scale the last three steps and meet Vic Bright and Eddie Young as they lead the way from the briefing room.

"Anything interesting?" Vic nods at my phone.

"Yeah, we've got a few banned lads down, drinking round Kings Cross."

"Everton at Arsenal?"

"No, unlikely. Some of ours have connections with them from England games. There's no history there. If anything goes off with them it'll be small groups of younger lads meeting by accident."

"Forest at Wimbledon?" Vic has done his homework.

"Yeah, they've got a good mob down apparently."

Vic reaches into his pocket and pulls out a black 6210.

"Do you know Paul Marsh, Forest's FIO?"

I shake my head and Vic flicks into the phone's address book and nods, then turns away and begins speaking into the phone so Young and I can't hear, and we hang around like spare parts as Inspector Bowen walks past and ignores us.

Vic Bright eventually turns back to face us and slides the phone into his pocket.

"Right, I've had a word with Paul. He knows the score, he can handle King's Cross. So, what are you expecting up here from your lot?"

Eddie Young has positioned himself alongside Vic and seems ready to speak so I take a step back and look at him.

"Erm...well our coaches will be mostly drinkers, we're not expecting any risk lads coming by bus. We know a couple are stopping at Redbridge, another couple at Dagenham."

"Right...and train?" Vic looks from Young to me and I keep my mouth shut. If Eddie's that fucking switched on then he can answer.

"Erm...probably a couple of hundred. The main risk group, erm, as we've said, will probably stay around King's Cross..."

I've proved my point, so I cough to signal that I'm about to bail him out.

"There are around forty Cat C targets currently drinking in the Mabel Tavern in Mabledon Place, including lads on banning orders. Some of this group plan to head to

Liverpool Street where they'll meet up with southern and midlands based Leeds supporters, a group which also includes a number of risk targets. From there, their intentions are unclear, but I'd guess they'll move by underground to Whitechapel or Mile End. Their aim will be to avoid getting wrapped up at Upton Park tube, so they'll most likely arrive at the ground just after kick off, probably by taxis."

Vic Bright is already nodding before I've finished and I decide to let him have his moment.

"What about your lot?"

"The ICF..." Eddie Young chips in and Vic raises his eyebrows.

"You've obviously been watching those hooligan DVDs they sell on the Internet."

Eddie smiles and nods and I stifle a snigger.

"The proper lads haven't called themselves ICF since about 1988. If anything, they call themselves Under-5's now." Vic flashes me a look and I shrug.

"The older lads will be drinking in Barking. It's beyond the exclusion zone so the banned lot can stay there when the rest go to the ground. If any of your coaches turn up there though, it's got potential."

"I doubt they will. As I said, they're all straight members, there's no risk bus today and I've told the supporters clubs to stop further out, but you never know."

Vic Bright nods and winks at a WPC leaving the briefing room.

"Our younger lads will be drinking near the ground - The Queens and Duke of Edinburgh on Green Street. We'll have bodies outside both, plus the Boleyn in case any of your shirters decide to pop in. Right, I'm going to have a ride out to Barking. We've got Man City away next week and I'm hearing there's a couple of naughty buses travelling. I want to have a sniff around, see what the plans are. Then I'll catch up with you at Liverpool Street. I'll get one of my lads to chauffeur you, don't want you getting lost in the big smoke do we?" Vic grins and slaps me on the shoulder then removes a pair of black leather gloves from his jacket pocket.

"Come on lads, I've a feeling it's going to be a busy day."

Chapter 3

Hamilton Hall, Liverpool Street station. The former ballroom of the Great Eastern Railway Hotel, now transformed into one of the cheapest sources of matchday ale in London by the rapidly expanding JD.Wetherspoon pub company. Golden chandeliers and rococo flourishes adorn the ceilings of the cavernous main bar, which today echoes with the accents of the north. Outside, a large patio area faces onto Bishopsgate, a perfect position for a firm of away fans to see and be seen, and around eighty Leeds lads have already colonised the space when we arrive in an unmarked car just after eleven.

"Just park up here for a minute and let's see what's what." I turn to the Met officer in the driver's seat and crane my neck to see who's outside.

"Tony M there. Steely. The twins from Lincoln." Eddie Young in my ear from the back seat. I make a mental note of who's wearing what, who's talking to who, who's there and who's not. None of Shivers' mob that I can see.

"Come on, lets a have a walk."

"I'll shift the car round the back and see you in there." The Met officer glances in the rear view mirror as we clamber out, EGT Pierre struggling with his camera bag on the back seat.

The fans outside the pub spot us approaching, and the ritual dance of football spotter and lads begins. As an approximate rule of thumb, 30% of supporters in an away pub will be straight members, probably pissed, enjoying a sing-song in their club shirts, more or less oblivious to your presence.

Another 30% are what I call 'Plod's Pals'– they need you to acknowledge them, call them by their name, maybe drop in a private joke or reference to a past event, let them feel important. Make sure everyone knows you know them, which means they're a top boy, one of the firm.

30% are the 'Hostiles'. They'll make a point of blanking you or maybe staring you out, or make some snide comment, maybe offer you a pork scratching to the amusement of their mates. This group will include a faction of proper criminals of varying levels, from weekend pub dealers to serious full time players. Most will have a record and many will have done time.

These groups account for the majority of away fans, but they aren't our main focus. Some will have a go if it comes on top, even more will pretend to, but only when they're behind a line of robocops. Most just want a decent drink and hope the football doesn't spoil the day out too much.

It's the remaining 10% that keep us on our toes. The so-called 'risk supporters'. The Cat C lads who will go looking for it. Who know their counterparts around the country by name, who have a mobile phone full of contacts as eager as they are to call it on. As soon as the fixtures come out, these lads will be checking who's playing where in the country on the same day, assessing the potential of a meet-up at some neutral venue, a pub near a railway station in a town whether neither team is playing, or like today, in a London backstreet well away from any football ground. Where no one expects it until it happens, then by the time the Met or BTP turn up, it's already over. A smashed-up boozer and a landlord who doesn't even know who the two mobs were.

It can be a proper needle-in-a-haystack job where the law are left chasing shadows. And that's where people like me come in. The football spotter, or to give the job its modern title, Football Intelligence Officer. My job is to know what's going to happen before it does. Those of us who are especially keen, like myself and my Manchester counterpart Lee Molloy, might even know it's going to happen before the lads themselves do. And to be able to do that, you need a relationship with the main lads. Fuck the drinkers, the Plod's Pals and the Hostiles, they're unimportant. You need to be speaking to the organ grinders, not the monkeys, and as I push open the glass doors of the Hamilton Hall, I'm scanning the room for one man. My organ grinder, Carl 'Shivers' Reed, so called because, according to legend, in advance of it kicking off, his hand trembles so much he spills his pint.

I push through the crowd, sensing the looming presence of Eddie Young behind me. I scowl at the hostiles, looking them up and down, noting jacket colours, trainers and cap brands; I nod and wink and smile at the 'pals', drop a few names and admire new coats and banter about past trips. A table from Donny, already pissed from the train, are in the mood for a sing-song.

'He's only a poor little cockney...bastard!'

Eddie Young slows down and glares at them, and I scan the room until I spot the brown Stone Island ice jacket always worn by Neil Gorman. He's standing in a crowd surrounding a table in the corner and I pause, peering through the crowd, ticking off the names – Ramsden, Steve Kenny, Husky, Big Paul Gilbert, and at the far side of the table, Shivers. He catches my eye and looks away. I wait until he looks back, then flick my eyes towards the gents and turn to see Eddie Young wagging his finger at the pissed Donny lads.

"Come on, we'll plot up outside, see if you can get some shots of lads coming and going." I point to the door and EGT Pierre follows me.

We stand at the far side of the courtyard, Eddie Young joins us and stares out each set of lads who emerge from the station. Pierre snaps away at everyone I point him to, collecting base evidence, in other words, who's wearing what, so if it kicks off later, we can match up clobber to culprits.

"I'll go check the bogs."

"Seen something?" Young starts to follow me but I shake my head.

"No, just need a piss. You wait here."

The bar is busier now and as I cross the room I glance across to the table in the corner. No Shivers.

I push open the toilet door, go along the corridor and up the steps, then down another corridor until I spot the fake-walnut door with a brass Gents sign. I open the door and glance down a row of traps, then walk along booting the doors open. Two lads emerge from one and freeze when they see me.

"Alright boys." I smile and they scurry out into the bar, nipping their nostrils. One door is still showing the red 'lock' symbol.

"Shivers?"

The lock slides back and the door squeaks open.

"Alright Millsy."

He's straight out, kicking open the other trap doors then reaching the door to the bar, he stands, foot against it, preventing anyone entering. He extends his right hand.

"Come on then, don't fuck about."

I reach into my jacket and pull out a white envelope and hand it over. He places it in the pocket of his Henri Lloyd jacket and thrusts a brown envelope towards me.

I tear open the envelope and remove a bundle of twenties and begin to flick through them. There's a slip of paper with a biro scrawl left in the envelope and I place it in my trouser pocket without looking at it.

"Fucks sake Millsy, you still don't trust us?"

"I don't trust anyone Shivers, especially you."

He smiles and taps the pocket of his jacket.

"These definitely right then?"

"They're what's on PNC. Last known. If they aren't still there, there's nowt I can do about that."

Shivers nods. "Let's hope they're good. Because there's not long to go now. When he gets out, I've a feeling we're all going to be busy."

He turns and pulls open the door.

"Where you lot heading?" I follow him into the corridor.

"Victoria Tavern at Plaistow. Cockney Dave knows the landlord. We'll get taxis from there after kick off. Has their copper said owt?"

"Not much. Their older lot are out at Barking. Doesn't sound like they're bothering."

"What's new Millsy, they never do..." he turns as I follow him to the top of the stairs.

"Hang back a bit mate, I don't want anyone seeing me talking to you. Not good for either of us, know what I mean?"

Chapter 4

"What's the mood like with your lot?"

Vic Bright turns only briefly in our direction, but doesn't respond immediately to Eddie Young's question. He's standing with his EGT Video and Still photographers outside the Queen's pub on Green Street, E13, monitoring the flow of supporters flooding from the Boleyn Ground, two hundred yards down the road.

"Mood? What do you mean?"

"Well, turned over 2-0 at home, Batty sent off for elbowing one of your players. Are they pissed off, likely to be out looking for it?"

Bright's impatience at Eddie's question isn't disguised, as he points his photographer towards three lads in baseball caps and goggle-hood jackets at a bus stop over the road.

"The ones who are looking for it won't give a fuck about the result. They'll be looking for it win, lose or draw. The rest are probably just looking forward to a pint."

I scan the crowd for familiar faces, but catch sight of the sign for the covered market next door and try to push the memories away. Shoppers scattering, stalls upturned, fruit and veg flying as we surprised the ICF on their own patch twenty years ago. I'm half tempted to ask Vic Bright if he was here that day, but they've opened the gates at the Leeds end and the first Strongbow shirts are appearing in the throng heading down the road, and Bright is barking orders into his radio.

"143, get your lads in position. Leeds to the right, West Ham to the left."

The radio crackles an inaudible response and Eddie Young follows Bright out into the road.

"Want me to go?"

Pierre the photographer is scrabbling with his camera, trying to change the film.

"No, wait with me. No point shifting unless something happens."

I watch Eddie and Bright pushing through the crowd, Eddie doing what he does, shoving people around, shouting, bullying, being a copper. That holds no interest for me. Any plod can whack someone with a baton. What I do is more specialised.

Less than five minutes have passed, and the majority of fans have now passed the pub and the market, and are queuing in two segregated masses on either side of Upton Park Tube Station. Green Street is still busy, but the slow march enforced by the shuffling crowd has given way to a normal walking pace and it's easier to see who's around.

"Come on." I tap Pierre on the arm and we turn left into the main road. My heart is beating faster and a surge of adrenaline makes my breath quicken. I recognise this feeling and welcome it like an old friend, but I know I have to use it, control it. I inhale through my nose as I walk, for a count of four. Hold for six. Exhale for four. Repeat. I'm scanning the street, ahead and behind me. I check out anyone not moving, standing, watching. My attention is drawn to specifics. Colours, haircuts, trainers, badges. I'm thinking like a hooligan now.

We pass the station on the other side of the road and I make sure I don't catch Eddie Young's eye. He's standing with the Leeds side of the queue, shouting, shoving, bullying. Pierre and I pass a Ladbrokes on a parade of shops on the right and I'm half tempted to call in to check the results. Leeds and Arsenal have won and I need to know the scores from Leicester and Huddersfield for my twenty quid Yankee. There's a Boots on the corner of a sidestreet called Harold Road, and I pause as my attention is drawn to a group standing by a row of phone boxes. Baseball caps and a couple of Stone Island tops but they're wearing grey joggers and chunky Nike trainers. Junior street dealers, chavs, not football lads. We carry on along the road, past discount shoe outlets, Iceland, Bombay Fashion House and countless Halal Butchers. First pub, the Duke of Edinburgh. A white painted single storey boozer on a corner. A few of their lads are in the doorway, a couple of them talking on mobile phones. I spot one of Vic Bright's lads and walk over.

"Anything interesting?"

"About fifty of our risk in here, mostly youth. Any of yours about?"

"Nothing yet. That's why I'm having a mooch." I give him a wink and look down the road.

"Forest Gate tube is this way isn't it? How long to walk?"

"Never done it but I'd say twenty, twenty five minutes. Plaistow is probably nearer."

Plaistow through the backstreets would have been my choice if I was looking for it, so we take a left at the next lights. It's a long straight road with side streets off to the left, which all lead back towards the ground and Upton Park Tube. This feels right, and I quicken my step, Pierre struggling to keep up with his bag of lenses. I'm glancing down every side road on the left, my heart beating fast. The streets are quiet now and I feel like a hunter stalking prey, sensing opportunity in open country. There's a shop selling second hand fridges on the corner of Dacre Road and a movement catches my attention as I stare down the avenue of pre-war semis and terraces. Two figures walking quickly. Jeans, trainers, tight dark coloured anoraks. I stop. Three more follow them, one carrying a beer bottle. Then five more, then a larger group I can't count, moving left to right on a side road which intersects ours.

"Come on."

I'm almost jogging now, with Pierre lagging fifteen feet behind me, and we reach the corner and I do a quick headcount. A good twenty five. I don't recognise anyone, but the way they're moving suggests they're Leeds and are unsure of the directions they've been given.

We follow, a hundred yards behind the group, the semis turning into boxy council houses and maisonettes. We pass a tyre shop. A fat man, his bare arms coated black with oil, emerges and opens the back doors of a van.

"Excuse me mate, what's the name of this road?"

He looks me up and down, taking in the kit and the high-vis and the cap with its WYP badge, then looks at Pierre with his camera bag, and I think he's going to tell us to fuck off.

"Crescent Road this. It's curved, like a crescent you see..."

I'm worried he's about to launch into a local history lecture so fire off my next question quickly.

"What's the nearest pub?"

The fat man walks from behind the van, rubbing his hands on an oil-slick towel.

"Pub? The Lamb at the end of the road. You don't want to go in there though...total shithole mate!"

I've got my mobile out before he's finished talking, and flick into the address book and locate Vic Bright. He answers straight away.

"PC Mills, nice of you to join us..."

"Do you know a pub called the Lamb, Plaistow way?"

I can hear the echo of chanting down the line and hope he hasn't got on a train.

"Yeah, estate pub, why?"

"There's a tidy mob of our risk lads about five minutes away. No law apart from me and the EGT lad."

"Fucking hell, right, see you there in a few minutes!"

We jog to catch up with the group who have slowed down at a junction. I can see the Lamb at the end of the road. Joined on to two council houses in the shadow of a tower block, it's a classic 70's estate pub. All that's missing is the flat roof with a barking alsatian on it. Two lads on phones outside the pub turn in our direction and see a clobbered-up firm approaching at speed, with a copper and a bloke with a camera bag fifty feet behind them. Unsurprisingly the lads look confused as they try to work out who it is that's about to pay them a visit.

I'm close enough to clock the Leeds lads now and recognise Paul Gilbert due to his height and the turquoise Berghaus coat he's wearing.

"Gilby...!"

The lads at the back of the mob turn and spot us and a couple stop in their tracks, but the lads at the front are focused on the pub, from where a dozen figures are now spilling out of the door, bottles and glasses in hand. I was expecting a roar and a charge from one of the two groups, but time seems to stand still as they size each other up, Leeds in a narrow road of parked cars and West Ham in the doorway of the pub. My guess is that Leeds are waiting to see what numbers the Londoners have, and West Ham know they don't have enough, so for a few seconds there's a stalemate which gives me time to make a move. I check that Pierre has his camera in hand then flick my baton and step forward.

Steve Kenny and a lad I don't recognise pull their hoods over their heads and swerve past us back up the road. They've all seen us now and there seems to be an equal split of annoyance and relief - The presence of the Old Bill gives everyone a free-pass in terms of lack of participation. West Ham certainly seem more confident now and a couple step forward into the road, arms raised, beckoning the Leeds lads forward. A young lad in a grey CP Company Urban Protection jacket steps out from the group and launches a bottle which smashes on the pub wall as the wail of sirens fills the street. The Leeds lads are backpedalling now, backing off down Crescent Road, but a TSG van screeches to a halt and disgorges a team of robocops with batons drawn, and our boys are quickly surrounded. West Ham are feeling brave and more have spilled from the pub and are standing, arms outstretched chanting 'Irons! Irons!' A counter chant of 'Leeds, Leeds, Leeds' competes with sirens and the barking of canine units from further down Crescent Road.

Pierre is snapping away at the kettled Leeds firm who respond with a mixture of wanker signs and hoods pulled over faces. I feel a hand on my shoulder and turn to see the grinning face of Vic Bright.

"Fucking hell mate, how long were you following this lot?"

Eddie Young is over his shoulder, scowling and shaking his head.

"Just followed my nose and found them. Call it copper's intuition."

Vic Bright snorts loudly and expels a gob of mucous onto the pavement, then leans in close and mutters under his breath.

"No son, that's not copper's intuition. I'd call it proper spotter intuition. Others might call it hooligan intuition."

He slaps me on the back and walks off towards the pub.

Chapter 5

'You don't have to do this.' The old man has bloodshot eyes and he smells of chemicals and decay. His face is close to mine and his nose and forehead shine with sweat. I try to speak but can only manage a hoarse whisper as I brush past him into a blood drenched kitchen. I feel my heart rate suddenly quicken and I struggle to catch my breath as my face flushes with a sudden infusion of blood. I inhale slowly through my nose, my senses struggling to stay in control, but a tide of nausea is rising from my stomach, and I have to swallow hard to suppress it. My hands are soaked in sweat and my knees begin to tremble. My heart feels like it will explode from my rib cage. I know this feeling well, this rising panic, the loss of control and I know I have to use it, observe it, stay in control. I close my eyes and breathe in through my nose for a count of four. Hold for six. Exhale for four. Repeat. And again. I feel my breathing begin to slow as I imagine the cold darkness of the water enveloping my body, the chill spreading from my feet, up my lower legs to my thighs. I shiver and inhale again, count to four. Hold for six. Exhale for four. The water is up to my chest now, ink black and dappled with chunks of ice. The cold makes me gasp as I inhale again and submerge my head. I open my eyes and blink at the shock of icy water, looking up as I sink down into the black depths, my heart rate slowing along with my breathing. Lower and deeper I sink, watching as the sunlit panel of sky shrinks away into the gloom above me. I'm blind now and alone, and the sounds and smells of the world above the surface are gone. I open my mouth to let the cold, black water fill it, I taste the toxic liquid on my tongue and *drink it in, until it replaces the oxygen in my lungs. My heart has stopped beating now, my breathing still, my body shut down. I'm where I need to be, back in control. I turn to the man and say 'where is she?' He smiles and a red tear trickles down his cheek.*

"Fuck!" I pull back the sweat-soaked duvet and sit up in bed, then scrabble in the darkness for the packet of Marlboro and a lighter. I hold my Tag Kirium up in front of my nose and squint at the fluorescent green hands. 5.22. I rub at my temples and try to work out what day it is, then feel a familiar sinking in my stomach. Fucking Monday morning and I'm on duty in a couple of hours.

Chapter 6

"Shit." My voice has a sandpaper edge and the knuckles of my right hand are swollen, making it hard to retrieve my wallet from my police issue cargo trousers, as I vainly search out a companion for the single twenty pound note remaining in there.

"Bollocks." I try to remember how much cash I had before I got the two-fifty from Shivers, to calculate how much I've managed to spunk away at the bar and bookies since Saturday. A lot. A fucking lot. I thrust a painfully swollen hand into the inside pocket of my jacket and remove a slip of paper with a biro scrawl. Three more names. Another couple of hundred quid. I look at my bruised hand and try to remember how I did it. I look back at the names on the scrap of paper and wonder what's happened to the last lot. What will happen to this latest three. Fuck them. Not my problem. Live by the sword and all that. Sleep with dogs you get fleas.

I shuffle in my seat in the corridor and flex my fingers, enjoying listening to them crack, above the distant click of a keyboard and the insistent clang of an unanswered phone. The door in front of me opens and a middle-aged woman with short purple hair leaves the room and calls over her shoulder at me.

"He says you can go in."

I stand and grimace, straightening my jacket, then bend and rub at a scuff of mud on my boots. I straighten up and immediately feel dizzy, steadying myself on the frame before I push open the door and enter Chief Inspector Tony Hudson's office. He's staring at a large white computer monitor on his desk and doesn't acknowledge me as I enter, tapping away with a single finger on his keyboard. I feel my mouth twitching into a smirk. Classic seventies plod training. Establish ascendancy, belittle the subject. He expects me to cough to announce my presence, so I stand in silence and glance around the room. A cluster of framed photos balance on a filing cabinet. A young family, pretty blonde twenty something mother and crew-cut outdoors type dad and two little kids. The boy has lost his front teeth and I wonder if they'll grow back like his grandad's. Another frame surrounds Tony Hudson, sweating in an open necked shirt, eyes flash-red, receiving a trophy from an old bald bloke with glasses. Tony Hudson in a dinner jacket and a woman in a low-cut red dress. A pig and his pig wife. Anniversary or Christmas dinner. On the wall a framed citation that I can't read. On the other wall, another certificate that I can't read, but at the top I spot the square and compass. Not an anniversary or Christmas dinner. A pig and his pig wife at a lodge meeting. Tony Hudson, second degree mason, his snout in the trough with the rest of them.

"PC Mills..." He stops tapping on the keyboard and slowly diverts his attention from the screen, motioning with his eyes for me to sit.

I slowly and painfully pull out a fake leather swivel chair and shake sweaty hands with myself under the desk.

"How was the weekend?"

I contemplate whether to tell him that I went straight from the last London train to Square on the Lane, then to the Duncan, then Café Inseine, then Oporto on Call Lane where I lost my rucksack. Then that I slept on the bar at Po-na-na behind the Corn Exchange, got woken up by the cleaners, then had another hour's kip in the doorway of William Hills at Beeston before they opened. I then spent most of Sunday in there, where I blew every penny I had, bar a twenty pound note which had got lost in the folds of my wallet. I then realise he's talking about West Ham away.

"It went okay sir. I managed to intercept a risk group en-route to a West Ham pub after the game, apart from that nothing major."

"Hmmm, very good, very good." Hudson taps away on the keyboard again with a single finger, then wrinkles his nose in disgust and shakes his head at something he's looking at on the screen.

"Anyway, you'll be wondering why I wanted to see you..."

I nod, trying to look like I care.

"Well, you'll be pleased to hear that following our meeting on Friday in Wakefield regarding the Manchester United game, it has been decided not to pursue the allegations made against yourself and PC Molloy."

I nod again. Lee Molloy, right as usual.

"It was felt that there was no conclusive evidence to support any of the claims made, so the matter won't be taken any further, but it will be left on file."

"The right decision sir I think." I smile and am about to stand up when Hudson raises his left index finger and points to the chair.

"I'm not finished yet PC Mills."

I slowly lower myself back onto the fake leather seat and Tony Hudson regards me with obvious distaste, blinking quickly and retracting his top lip to reveal his stunted yellow teeth.

"I won't beat about the bush here PC Mills, I'm not one for dancing around my handbag as it were..." He smiles at his stolen use of Ken Baxter's phrase.

"I'm not going to pretend that I was happy when you were assigned to our FIO role when Malcolm moved on, I had my own thoughts on who should get the job..."

Yeah, Eddie fucking Young's arse-licking style was right up your street.

"But when the ACC made me aware of your circumstances, I had no hesitation in stepping forward to assist in your rehabilitation."

You mean my old boss told your boss you had to have me. My boss outranked your boss, so you had no fucking say in the matter.

"You've been in role for nearly ten months now..." He pauses and tilts his head to the left like a curious spaniel, clearly expecting me to speak. I stay silent and tilt my head to the right, avoiding his eyes and staring at his teeth.

"You'll remember that an important element of your joining us was that your...recovery...would be aided by the excellent mental health facilities offered by our Occupational Health Service."

I nod gently and slowly, so that Hudson seems unable to decide whether I'm nodding or not.

"You do recall that PC Mills?"

"Mmmmm." I nod and push out my bottom lip.

"You recall that a recommendation of your joining us...no actually, I'll re-phrase that...a condition of your joining us was that you would attend regular sessions with an OHS approved counsellor to address your diagnosed PTSD and anxiety issues. Do you recall that?"

I know what's coming, and inhale deeply then puff out my cheeks and exhale loudly as Hudson starts turning pages in a file on his desk.

"You haven't attended a counselling session since February."

"Is it that long?" I'm surprised it's taken them two months to realise I haven't been going.

"Yes, 9th February was your last session."

"Yeah, well, the bloke was a...let's just say we didn't really get on. Anyway, I think I'm alright now."

Hudson is shaking his head before I've finished speaking.

"No, no, no...you aren't in a position to decide that. The OHS counsellor will make the decision on whether you still need support, and speaking quite candidly, from what I'm witnessing on a day to day basis, my personal opinion is that you are still a long way from 'alright' PC Mills."

I contemplate asking what the fuck he means by that, but then decide I can't be arsed, so I sink lower in my seat and stare at the desk.

Tony Hudson's hand appears in my line of sight, holding a white, rectangular card.

"You will ring this number as soon as you leave this office and you will make an appointment to see a counsellor this week." Hudson shakes the card until I reach out and take it.

"And I've asked the OHS to make me aware if they don't hear from you today. So make the call, then go to the appointment. It's for your own good."

You mean you'll get a bollocking if I go off on long term sick on your watch, and leave you shorthanded with a Champions League final on the cards.

I stand slowly and for a second I think I'm going to puke over Tony Hudson's desk.

"Is that all sir?"

Tony Hudson nods and waves his hand in the direction of the door.

"Yes, PC Mills, that's all. Now go make that call."

Chapter 7

"So what do you want to know?" He's in his early fifties, soft Irish accent and a thick mop of greying hair in a side parting, and a neat beard, greyer than the hair.

"Do you dye your hair?"

He smiles and pushes his glasses back up the bridge of his nose.

"No, why?"

"Your beard is whiter than your hair. Looks unnatural."

"If I dyed my hair, don't you think I'd dye my beard to match?" His blue eyes sparkle with mischief and he reminds me of someone, but I don't want to like him, so I try not to remember who. I look away and glance around the room. Classic psychiatrist refit of a high-ceilinged room in an old Victorian terrace in Hyde Park. An office chair sits behind a desk with a lamp and some files and one of those Newton's Cradle toys with the silver balls on strings, that every pseudo-intellectual had in the seventies. The thick dark curtains are partly drawn to try to block out the horrors of what's out there, what's brought people like me here, to see this grey haired loony-whisperer sitting opposite me in one of a pair of matching leather armchairs.

"Anything else you want to know about me then?"

"Isn't it meant to be you asking me the questions?" I glance at my watch, wondering if he's trying to trick me.

"Aye, well, that's how it usually works, but that always seems a little impolite to me. Why should you tell me anything if you know nothing about me?"

"Fair enough. Go on then, who are you?"

The Irishman pushes himself up from the armchair and crosses the room.

"Tea or coffee?"

I shake my head and he picks up a cup from a tray and pours himself one from a cafetiere on a small table by the window.

"My name is Noel Kelly. I'm fifty three and I'm a registered psychotherapist. I've done the job for eighteen years. I used to work in HR for the council in Cork. Moved over here when I got remarried...that didn't last. I live on my own in Roundhay now with two cats. I like rugby, proper rugby, not the type you play round here. Music, Springsteen, Fleetwood Mac. I like a beer, real ale, not overly keen on the black stuff if I'm honest." He sits down opposite me and smiles, blue eyes glinting again.

"So that's me really...anything else you'd like to know?" He seems amused by the whole situation, like he's playing a joke on himself. When he nods and his left eye briefly twitches into what could be either a tic or a wink, the half-memory flashes through my mind again and I remember my grandad. I dispel the thought. Keep your guard up. This bastard's clever, getting in your head. I shrug.

"So my turn now I suppose?"

Noel Kelly swivels in his seat and picks up a file from his desk and I glance across, expecting to see pages of notes, but the A4 sheet is blank.

"In your own time." Kelly picks up a pen from the desk and suspends it above the page as he sits down. "You don't mind if I take notes?"

I shake my head. "If it speeds things up, do what you want."

The room falls silent, apart from the faint tick of a carriage clock on a mantal piece above a sealed-up fireplace.

"Where should I start?" I hope he isn't going to do the earliest memory one or make me look at ink blots.

"Start wherever you want...why are you here?"

"Because my boss told me I had to."

"Why?"

"Because I'd been off sick then I got transferred up here. It was a condition of me coming back to work that I'd have counselling."

"Why were you off sick?"

The Irishman is good. No dancing round handbags with Noel Kelly.

"They said I had PTSD."

"Who said?"

"The Met doctors, counsellors, people like you."

"And why were you seeing those people in the first place?"

No dancing at all now, Noel Kelly has stopped the music and I can feel my heart beating hard.

"Something happened. Something bad."

Noel Kelly nods his head. The smile is still there but the mischief has gone from his eyes.

"Tell me what happened Charlie."

Chapter 8

"I worked for So10, what they call SCD10 now. Covert Policing Unit in the Met. I was a Level 1 undercover operative. One of the elite. One of the top ten undercover officers in the country."

As soon as I've said it, I feel my heart rate quicken and I struggle to catch my breath. I know this feeling well. I feel my face flush and I can tell Noel has noticed too. I inhale slowly through my nose, trying to stay in control. My hands are soaked in sweat and my knees are trembling. I close my eyes and breath in through my nose for a count of four. Hold for six. Exhale for four. Repeat. I feel my breathing begin to slow as I imagine the cold darkness of water enveloping my body, the chill spreading from my feet, up my lower legs to my thighs, then to my body and over my head.

"Do you want a drink?"

Noel Kelly pulls himself up from his chair and crosses the room, slowly pouring a glass of water from a jug with clinking ice cubes that's on the table near the window.

"I'm sorry, I don't feel great. I might just go." I stand and expect Kelly to object, but he smiles and hands me the glass of water, and I remember once as a kid being sick and my grandad stood in my bedroom doorway doing exactly the same, and I sit down again.

The only sound in the room is the ticking of the clock and my heaving breath and Noel Kelly's biro scratching on the paper in his file. I breathe in through my nose for a count of four. Hold for six. Exhale for four.

"Take your time."

"Yeah so...SCD 10. Undercover...deep undercover. Not the sort of job where you go home to your family every night. This is about playing a long game. You have to build a credible backstop, get new bank accounts, National Insurance number, property rental history, police record, everything. You live on your plot full time. You work there, shop there, drink there. I'm talking about months, years sometimes. Living your legend they call it. You have to actually become the person you're pretending to be..."

I'm speaking too quickly, too eager to get the words out. Noel Kelly doesn't speak, doesn't look up from his scribbling.

"This is completely confidential right?" There's a voice in my head screaming what the fuck are you doing, but it suddenly feels easier to say it than not to, so I carry on at a hundred miles an hour.

"It was a multi-agency op. Easier to say who wasn't involved than who was. NCS, NCIS, Europol, CTC and just about every other fucking three letter agency you could think of was in on it. Lots of fingers in the pie. The target was an OCG, Kurdish mafia with links to the PKK. My legend was that I ran a hardware shop, I was ex-army, Royal Engineers. I had a workshop in Kilburn where I converted and re-activated firearms for the Kurdish and Turkish gangs across North London. I established links with paramilitary groups in the Balkans, and the job was to bring a big shipment of hardware in via Tilbury docks for the Kurds. Major league stuff."

"How long were you in the field?"

"In total, including establishing the backstop, the op had been ongoing for nearly seven months when..." I feel the panic rising again and pause, waiting for the icy water to reach my chest and slow my heart, which is thumping so hard it's making my rib cage ache.

"Take your time...so you'd been undercover that whole time, away from your family?"

"As I said, this was deep undercover. You can't risk breaking the legend, not even for a couple of hours. The risk of being seen somewhere you shouldn't be was too high. Also, it's easier that way. You can't just turn the legend on and off. As I said, you have to actually become that person."

"And you were married?"

I nod and feel my lip start to tremble and my eyes prickle.

"We had a daughter...have a daughter. She's eight." I place my right hand on my chest and push down on my ribs, trying to stop my heart bursting out of my shirt.

Noel Kelly pushes his glasses up from the tip of his nose and taps his biro on the bristles on his chin.

"Okay, carry on... when you're ready."

"So...I was in for just over six months. My partner was Keeley, on the job I mean, not my wife..."

"Keeley was an undercover operative too?"

"Yes, Keeley was my wife in the legend. She worked in the restaurant the Kurds operated from. It was her who put them onto me. We lived together for six months as man and wife...it was hard. Fucked up, totally fucked up." I shake my head and breathe deeply as I stare at my feet.

"You became close?"

I laugh and rub my forehead with a sweat soaked palm.

"Yeah...you could say that. We had an affair. Didn't mean to. She'd just got married. In that situation though...what you're doing every day, the two of you...it's fucked up, as I said, the whole thing."

I raise my hands to my face and rock gently in my seat.

"Are you okay to carry on or do you want a break?"

If I stop now, If I come up for air, I know I'll never go back down again. I have to carry on.

"They killed her."

Just the ticking of the clock and my breathing now. Noel Kelly has stopped scratching on his pad.

"Go on..." His voice is quiet, as if he doesn't really want to hear.

"The cover was blown. Don't know how, think they had someone on the inside at Europol, everyone knows they're as leaky as fuck. That's the only way they could have known. Anyway, they came looking for me at the workshop, but I'd gone down to the docks to meet the Serbs. Keeley was at the restaurant..."

"You were lucky." As soon as he's said it, he knows he's fucked up, and raises his hands in mock surrender, expecting me to blow up. All I can do is laugh.

"Lucky...yeah, that's me, Noel. They tried to stop me going to the restaurant after, but I had to see her. She was in the deep freeze, in plastic bags. They'd cut her fingers and toes off while she was alive. Ears, nose, lips... tits of course..."

"My God." Noel Kelly has covered his mouth and nose with his hands and closed his eyes.

"I was pulled out and de-briefed, then given a month special leave. The op collapsed, no arrests. I went from being a full time gangster to a family-man copper overnight. I was in bits. Couldn't eat or sleep and Gemma, my wife, just didn't get it. So I told her about me and Keeley. I think I must have thought she'd feel sorry for me."

"It must have been terrible for her too. How did she react?"

"She kicked me out, there and then. I even said I'd leave the unit, stop the undercover work, but we were done. She wants a divorce, got a new bloke now I think. Won't even let me see my daughter... So do you still think I'm lucky Noel?"

He shakes his head, and I have to stop myself feeling sorry for him.

"I shouldn't have said that."

"Don't worry about it." I stand up and rub the sweat from my hands onto my Paul Smith jacket. "But lucky isn't a word you can really use to describe me."

"No, after what you've gone through, what I said was unforgiveable..."

I smile. "That's not the half of it Noel. Wait till you hear the rest." I walk to the door and turn the handle without looking back, catching his voice as I leave.

"See you next week, Charlie."

Chapter 9

Football intelligence. What they called a spotter in the old days. Back in the seventies it was a free-for-all. Lads in flares and feather-cuts kicking lumps off each other on the terraces and in town centres every weekend. You got nicked or you got away with it. If you were unlucky, some heavy handed plod with a porn-tash might remember you the week after and give you a clip round the ear, but that would be it. No CCTV, no undercover ops, dawn raids, prison sentences or banning orders. Simpler times.

Then came the eighties. Thatcher's national drive towards aspiration and enterprise spread to the football terraces. Club scarves and denim jackets covered in patches, gave way to golf jumpers, straight-leg Levis and expensive trainers. The law thought they were on top of things by taking the laces out of the Skinheads' boots, while the real thugs strolled out of the station carrying umbrellas and wearing deer-stalker hats.

While Gold Commanders across the country focused their resources on the chanting masses pouring off the football specials, the proper lads slipped quietly off the service train and melted away into the Saturday shoppers. No noise, no colours, anonymous to everyone except those who shared their code, those who were 'in the know.' The clothes, the hairstyle, what they wore on their feet, all were instantly recognisable to other groups of what became known as dressers, casuals, scallies, townies or perry boys, depending on where in the country you lived. The streets and decaying football stadia of the early eighties became a stage for the actors in an ongoing drama referred to as the 'English Disease' by an over-excited and increasingly outraged media. The police were struggling to adapt, and the tabloid press stoked the flames with talk of 'organised firms' controlled by 'shadowy generals' running riot in towns throughout Britain.

Something had to give and the riots at Luton, Birmingham and Heysel, plus the Valley Parade fire, were the multiple blood-splashed straws that finally broke the camel's back. Thatcher was on the warpath, and Home Secretary Douglas Hurd made it clear to the Chief Constables that a new approach was needed. The seventies tactics of big boots and truncheons wouldn't cut it anymore. Intelligence led policing was the way forward, using tactics employed against the IRA, CND and the miners. Plain clothes officers would infiltrate the firms, win their confidence, share their plans and if necessary, instigate offences which could then be punished in high profile criminal trials. These were the golden days of football intelligence, and West Yorkshire Police were at the forefront of it with covert ops named Wild Boar and post-riot mop-ups like Operation Unrooley.

But that was fifteen years ago, and the world had changed. The technological revolution had seen to that. In the mid-eighties, a copper doing my job would have spent his working week as a beat-bobby who would then devote a few hours to pre-match planning on a Friday morning, then spend Friday night touring the right pubs in town - Jac's, Spencers, Yates's, Harlequins. Saturday would have been spent on Boar Lane and Mill Hill, chasing lads in bleached jeans and Italian tracksuit tops or later, flared cords and Peter Storm cagoules. Twelve thousand at the average Leeds home game would have contrasted sharply with two thousand on every away trip, 95% of whom were lads under the age of twenty five who were all dressed alike and weren't necessarily there for the champagne football dished up at Elland Road in the early eighties.

Trips to Madrid, Milan and Barcelona must have seemed like an impossible dream to matchday coppers back in those days, and I smile as I apply blue-tac to the back of a postcard which I then stick to the bottom of the white computer monitor on my desk. An aerial view of the Spanish city of A Coruña, placed alongside others from Spain and Italy, Istanbul and Brussels.

"Good trip last week?" Helen, a WPC with copper-coloured hair scraped back into a tight bun, leans over me and peers at the Roman lighthouse sat on a peninsula alongside the old town.

"Usual...didn't see much of it really. Don't tell Youngie that though."

Helen laughs as she walks across to her own desk. "Yeah, he's still well pissed off about getting bumped. Keep rubbing it in."

I flick at the mouse and screw up my eyes in response to the harsh blue light which floods the monitor screen as a flickering West Yorkshire Police logo appears.

I sign in and click an icon on the desktop, sitting back in my chair to watch the egg-timer icon begin to spin as the website slowly loads, to the buzz and whine of the internet dialling up. My baby. LeedsSC.Org. The Service Crew message board, the second most visited hooligan message board in the country. I wait until the banner at the top of the page loads, a nice professional touch I feel, I got one of the IT lads to design it for me. I then click the 'log in' command at the top right-hand side of the page.

The terminal under my desk whirrs and clicks and eventually the log-in prompt turns into *'Welcome - Administrator.'*

I start to scroll through the new posts, looking for any mention of Chelsea next Saturday. The DPP guidance on covert hosting of hooligan message boards is imprinted in my brain – *'Sanctioned for the purposes of intelligence gathering only. Planning or discussion of future disorder on police-hosted message boards and forums constitutes entrapment and is strictly prohibited in any form.'*

Any posts talking about what's potentially going to happen at a future game therefore have to disappear immediately, to prevent any future evidence from the board being compromised. Obviously not until I've copied them and noted the email address of the poster though.

I scroll down through the posts, but no one seems to be talking about next week. There are two new user requests which I authorise, then add the details to an Excel spreadsheet.

User name - KnottlaWhite – mhinchliffe@btinternet.co.uk

User name – PaulLUFC3 – paulwalker6548@yahoomail.com

I click on the icon for the Police National Computer, and open up a notepad on my desk to reveal a list of passwords. Less than five minutes later I'm looking at a photo of Martin Hinchliffe, date of birth 7/10/1966, one conviction for breach of the peace in 1988. I add his address and a copy of his photo to my spreadsheet. Paul Walker seems to be a clean skin, no record, assuming

6/5/48 is his date of birth. Old bloke anyway. Hardly likely to be a new major player at his age.

I flick down through the posts on the service crew forum. The usual stuff. Drinking in town in the eighties; Someone trying to shift an Arsenal away ticket; Price of flights to Alicante; Newcastle turning up in Harehills in the seventies; a couple of shit jokes; Phoenix Nights on the telly; Albert Johanneson; Going to 80's away games in tranny vans.

Half way down the page, one post catches my eye. 'Plaistow on Saturday.' I click into it.

TopTableSC – Heard some of ours had a bit of a wander after the match...

Birstall – We had it with them just round the corner from the tube. 10 of us, about 30 of them.

TopTableSC- Was that before?

Birstall – About 5 minutes before kick off.

TopTable SC – Was that black cunt of the documentary with them?

BelleIsle10 – He was mouthing it outside the turnstile before.

Interesting, as this seems to have gone under the radar. Could be bullshit but I make a note of the user names.

Birstall – we tried to get down to that Duke of Edinburgh after forty of us. OB on horses took us back to the tube.

TopTableSC- Heard West Ham had given pub name to a cockney white. Good 30 got down there but law were there quick.

Birstall- How many West Ham?

TopTableSC -Pub full I heard but they didn't come out till OB turned up. Our lot got S60'D.

BelleIsle10 – Was CM there?

TopTableSC – What do you think? He was already at pub when they got there.

Birstall- Knows too much that cunt. Someone's talking.

I flick back to my Excel spreadsheet and filter on the three user names then add a note to each – *potential involvement in minor disorder, West Ham 21/4/01*. Then I delete the thread.

I close the Service Crew board down and click on another icon on the desktop. This one takes longer to load, due to a combination of Holbeck nick's steam powered internet and a more high-tech website design. ITK is Britain's most visited hooligan message board with over twenty thousand registered users from just about every team in the country and beyond. It supposedly took the Met's tech support team two months to build, due to a clever feature that means all users have to be 'vouched for' by an existing member. That helps restrict the membership to the main players. As the name suggests, only those who are actually 'in the know' are able to join. It also provides the Met's monitoring team with a complex spider's web of hooligan alliances. Who's talking to who, which firms have links, who's fallen out with who. The Private Message function also allows lads to correspond off the main board, to discuss what's happened and, more importantly, what's going to happen, where and when. As they're not on a public forum, the thinking is that the messages fall into a grey area of the DPP guidance, though no one has actually tried to test this theory in court yet.

There are around ten Leeds lads on the ITK site, who all seem suspicious of running their mouths on the board or in private messages. Fortunately, Lee Molloy's lads are less careful, and the Met lads have had to delete a few posts from Man Utd lads relating to the 'Battle of Holbeck' in the run up to the recent court cases. I flick into the 'General' board and scroll down looking for anything from my lads or any posts from West Ham or Chelsea. All's quiet on the internet front. Clearly West Ham are choosing to keep quiet about Leeds turning up at one of their pubs at the weekend.

I stand up and walk to the window, looking out across Burton Road to the 'Crop Shop' barber's on the redbrick corner of Fairford Terrace. I turn back to the room and watch Helen's red pony tail bobbing above her computer terminal. At the far side of the room, a plump lad called Stuart sits with his feet on the desk, occasionally muttering into a phone cradled under his chin, the curled cable stretched taut in front of him. I look back out of the window, scanning the car park for Eddie Young's red escort.

I walk back to my desk and sit down, then click into PNC and select the option to log out. I open the notepad and run my finger down the list of user names and passwords until I find 'edwardyoung'. Helen is tapping away on her keyboard but as I begin to enter Eddie Young's details into the PNC log-on screen, a desk phone begins to ring across the office. I duck my head, my heart beating faster.

"I suppose I'll get this then lads..." Helen stands and stomps noisily across the office as I reach into my shirt pocket and pull out the scrap of paper with three names scrawled in biro.

"No, he's not in yet...not sure." Helen is leaning on the desk facing me, looking across the room. I duck my head lower as PNC opens on the screen in front of me.

"...243 7698. Okay. Yeah, I'll tell him." Helen writes on a pad on the desk then drops the pen and walks back across the room as I type the first name into PNC.

An address in Wakefield. Possession with intent to supply, various charges. Burglary, shop lifting. Probably a minor dealer who owes them money. I write the address next to the name on the piece of paper.

Next name, last known address in Morley but that's from four years ago. Same profile – drugs, theft, assault. No chance he'll still be there. Whatever he's done, he's probably got away with it. I write down the address.

Final name. Released from Armley last week to an address in Huddersfield. Bigger player, served four years for conspiracy to supply a controlled substance. Cleared of firearms charges. I look at the name again. Malik Ishmael. 30/6/77. I've got a bad feeling about this one, but fuck him. You live by the sword and all that. I write down the address, then put the piece of paper back in my shirt pocket.

I look up to see Helen watching me with her arms folded.

"Tough gig eh Millsy?"

"What?" I click the mouse to close down the screen.

"Fucking about on your football forums all day then booking your next flight to Spain. It's a hard life innit?"

I smile. "It's called intelligence Hel...You've either got it or you haven't!"

"Yeah right...want a cuppa?"

"Go on then." I wink at her and click the mouse as she turns and walks away, then select 'log out' on the PNC screen and sign Eddie Young out of the system.

Chapter 10

"My younger brother and me, we killed our parents, then I killed my brother." If I'm expecting some sort of dramatic reaction from Noel Kelly, I'm going to be disappointed.

The blue eyes blink behind the lenses of his glasses, but the half-amused, half-bemused semi-smile remains. Clearly he's seen this 'throw-him-off-guard' tactic many times before. Noel Kelly licks at his lips and nods gently, his biro tapping on a blank page in his file.

"I'll assume you're not talking literally there Charlie..."

I shrug and look at my feet.

"So go on, tell me why you think that?"

I don't look up, but rub my sweat soaked palms on my jeans then sit on my hands to stop my fingers twitching.

"I don't think it, it happened."

Noel Kelly doesn't speak. He sits back in his chair, tilting his head, just weighing me up. Eventually he raises his eyebrows in a clear invitation to carry on with my story.

"1973. I was eight. Andy, my brother, would have been six. We'd been to Scarborough. This was before the A64 was a dual carriageway. No by-passes round Tadcaster and Malton then, you had to go through all the little villages on the way. It was August, school holidays. We never went away for a for a full week though, the old man was always too busy. Never had time for stuff like that. Anyway, I assume my mother had nagged him into a day-trip. A Saturday it was. Typical August weather. Sunny in the morning when we set off, cloudy and cold by the time we got there. We did the usual stuff. Walked along the beach, went on the rowing boats at Peasholm Park, played on the Penny Falls and the air hockey at Jimmy Corrigan's amusements. I remember we walked along to Valley Bridge and my dad made us look up at it, then told us how many people jump off it every year. I remember me and our kid looking up and asking how long we'd have to wait before someone threw themselves off. I can remember my dad laughing, probably because he didn't do that very much."

Noel Kelly looks like he's about to speak, probably to ask me about my relationship with my dad, my earliest memory of him, whether I loved him, the usual psychological digging, but he checks himself, smiles and nods, indicating that I should carry on.

"So, yeah...a day at the seaside. The Yorkshire Riviera, I can't remember much else about it. I think we got fish and chips, ate them at the harbour, I seem to remember being on a big wheel that was really small at one point, feeling embarrassed. My mum and dad went in that Newcastle Packet pub on the front for a drink and left me and our kid in Corrigan's arcade. Then we were in the car driving home. A Vauxhall Viva estate it was. My mum and dad in the front, me and Andy in the back. It was getting dark. I can vaguely remember car headlights coming towards us, me and Andy scrapping on the back seat, I had him in a headlock and he was screaming. 'Submit! Submit!' We used to play at wrestling, I was Mick McManus, he was Kendo Nagasaki, and that was the signal to stop. Only this time I didn't, I squeezed tighter, and he screamed louder. My mum was twisting round in the front, trying to get hold of me. I was pissing myself laughing, eight years old, little bastard I was. I remember my dad, half-turning and saying 'If I have to stop this bloody car lad, you won't sit down for a week.' I can picture his face, his lips curled back below his moustache, his arm reaching over the seat, trying to grab me. Then this bright light, he became a silhouette, then a flash, and a taste of petrol in my mouth. Next thing I knew I woke up in hospital. York General. Breathing tube in my nose, wires on my head and chest. I remember there was a little blonde lass in the bed next to me, all wrapped in bandages. She'd fallen into a bonfire on a farm. I can still remember the smell..."

Noel Kelly coughs and shuffles in the seat opposite me and I look at him, realising I've been staring at my feet for the last few minutes.

"She died. The girl in the bed next to me. Couple of hours after I woke up, they pulled the curtains round her bed and I could hear her mam and dad crying."

"And your parents and brother?" Noel Kelly speaks quietly and I can hear him breathing through his nose.

"Andy was okay, he had a broken leg but they'd discharged him by then. I'd been unconscious for ten days. They thought I'd be brain damaged if I ever woke up. Maybe they were right eh?"

I smile but Noel Kelly doesn't.

"Your parents?"

"Both killed instantly. Hit a Bedford Van, head on. We were on the wrong side of the road. The van driver lost both his legs."

I look at him for a reaction but his face remains impassive.

"I guess there was an inquest?"

I smile. "Yeah, they said my dad was over the limit, but he can't have had more than three in the time we were playing on the Penny Falls. He could easily drive on double that. He was good at drink driving, that's what he used to say to my mum. Me and Andy weren't even called as witnesses. They got our teacher to ask us what had happened, then she went to court and read out our statements."

"And what did you say had happened?"

I stare, unblinking into Noel Kelly's blue eyes and tell him what he already knows.

"We said we were asleep. We had no idea what happened. We were hardly likely to tell them that we caused it were we? That was mine and Andy's secret. We killed our parents. Then I killed him too."

Chapter 11

I flick open the Marlboro Lights packet and pull out the last cigarette with my teeth, light it and blow the smoke at my own reflection in the grimy pane of glass looking out onto the Headrow. I stare at the blue Hill's betting slip in my hand. A twenty quid Trixie which looked like coming off yesterday afternoon, until Crystal Lass letting me down in the last race at Southwell turned a £261 return into £28.

I place the slip back into my wallet and extend my right hand towards the half glass of Carling on the scuffed mahogany table, then stop myself. I tap my pocket to remind myself that I've just spent my last pound coin, and can't afford another drink until I go to the bookies. I check my watch as the speaker in the corner crackles into life. 12.45 on a Tuesday. Steady lunchtime trade is the best that most city centre pubs can hope for, but time doesn't apply in the Three Legs. No one in here has a job, unless you class grafting and shoplifting as a career. Few of the punters are ever sober enough to experience anything resembling a hangover. Every day is Saturday night, and the seventy year old with the purple nose who has hauled himself onto the raised step which serves as a stage, licks his cracked lips in anticipation. The karaoke machine buzzes and the lights pulse and he turns to face the room, as the lyrics to 'The Wonder of You' appear on a blue screen behind him. A toothless thirty year old woman with the face of a grandma, cackles and lurches and spins at the bar as her smackhead boyfriend looks on.

The sudden explosion of bass from the speaker causes the bus queue outside the window to turn towards the open door. Two old lasses snigger and smirk and one retrieves a leather purse from her pocket and furtively shows it to her friend and nods at the pub. The Three Legs, a Leeds institution. Source of stolen socks, gloves, leather goods and anything vaguely portable for as long as anyone can remember.

"Fuck me, I thought Elvis were dead." Shivers appears next to my table, fingers in his ears. "What you drinking?"

"Pint of Stella."

He looks at the half glass of Carling on the table and smirks and shakes his head as he walks to the bar, dodging the toothless disco dancer.

I swill down the last of my drink and suck on the Marlboro as Shivers turns back from the bar carrying two pints of lager.

"You got them then?" He pulls up a stool and sits down.

"You got my money?

"Skint again Charlie?" He laughs and passes a brown envelope over the table, as I hand him a folded slip of paper which he puts straight into the pocket of his jeans.

I count the cash and slip it into my jacket, sensing him lean in closer across the table.

"You won't need to worry about cash from now on anyway."

I look up and smell the beer and cigs on his breath from six inches away.

"Danny's brief has had the word. Release date is this Friday and he wants to hit the ground running when he gets out."

I feel my heart rate quicken as I'm transported back fifteen years. The Chained Bull, Penny Fun, Foxes. The Warehouse, House Music. What they called the second Summer of Love, only it wasn't that in LS17. Danny Cade. A milk-drinking body builder with a 2-litre black Capri. Connected and dangerous from the day he got kicked out of Allerton Grange at fifteen. Moved into weed and took on the blacks at Harvey's before he was old enough to buy a pint in there. Saw the potential for pills a year before Acid House arrived and wiped everyone else out before they'd even got started. Imported top of the range hardware from the Balkans when everyone else was trying to get hold of sawn-offs. Ran everything in north and west Leeds and was moving east when things got messy. Wanting a job done properly and deciding to do it himself was his downfall, when he was caught at the Shaftesbury traffic lights with a loaded Uzi, heading to a house in the Dawlish's to take the east Leeds underground crown from the head of Marlon Hopper. The kid in the car with him took the hit for the gun and the attempt murder charge, but Millgarth OCU weren't letting Danny walk free and he landed a six year sentence for aiding an offender. That was in '95. He served the full term, and now Danny Cade was on his way back. They say that chaos loves a vacuum, and the lack of any single dominant force in the Leeds criminal underworld had led to a splintering of factions and constant territorial battles at the end of the nineties. Word was that Danny Cade sensed an opportunity and he intended to take it. Quickly.

"So what's he want?"

Shivers glances over his shoulder and grimaces as the toothless junkie joins Elvis in a screeched finale to his party piece. He reaches into the pocket of his Henri Lloyd coat and retrieves a folded slip of paper and hands it over.

I open it and skim read the eight names, recognising a couple. I inhale sharply like a plumber assessing a badly blocked toilet.

"Some big names on there Shivers. A lot of names too."

He nods. "Aye, well, you've got a pay rise. Ton a name."

Eight hundred quid for a couple of minutes work. Can't argue with that.

"When do you need it by?"

"As soon as. But definitely before Saturday. We've got a box for Chelsea. Danny's homecoming party. He'll be wanting to see some progress by then."

I nod and Shivers swills down a third of his pint.

"Are you hearing owt about that? They bringing many?"

"I've not had my call with their spotter yet. Will let you know what he says."

Shivers shakes his head. "They'll do fuck all as usual. Their coppers know what they're doing before most of their lads do and that suits them. They'll get wrapped up before they land anywhere near, then give it the usual load of bollocks...we had a couple of hundred but 'law sussed it. Fucking bullshit."

"You could wait for the train at Wakey." I smile and mime lighting and throwing a petrol bomb.

Shivers grins and picks up his pint.

"I remember that. 82 was it? Or 83? They got some serious time for that those lads. Them were the days though eh Charlie?"

"So I've heard. Bit late for me that, I was more or less done with it all by then."

Shivers throws back the last of his pint and puts the glass on the table then leans towards me and winks.

"Bullshit Charlie. You're never done with it, you know that. You're still firm, you just don't wear the gear anymore."

I down my pint and put the slip of paper in the pocket of my jeans as a I stand up and smile at Shivers.

"You're right mate, I am still firm, just not yours. I'm part of the biggest firm in the country, and when it comes to football, we always win!"

Chapter 12

"How many hours do you usually sleep a night?"

Noel Kelly removes his glasses and rubs them slowly on his green M&S crew neck without looking at me.

"Sleep? Not many."

"Give me a number." Noel Kelly breathes on the lenses and holds them up to the shaft of light escaping through the gap in the curtains.

"Four, three maybe. I've spent my life working irregular hours. It fucks up your sleep patterns."

Noel Kelly nods. "Your circadian rhythms."

"I've never liked reggae."

He half smiles politely at my half joke.

"And drinking?"

I shrug and hold out my hands.

"Yeah, guilty."

"How much, and what?"

"Depends what I can afford but I don't do spirits. If I'm skint and I can't sleep I'll have a couple of bottles of Frosty Jack."

"A couple of 2 litre bottles?"

"It's only a quid."

"8% is it?"

"Don't get carried away Noel...7.5." I'm getting to know him now and am enjoying recognising the small signs. He knows to avoid any obvious disapproval, but I notice the slight downward eyebrow twitch, the tightening of his lips.

"Drugs?"

"That's probably the only vice I'm clean on. Fucked my brother up, so I won't have owt to do with them."

Noel Kelly nods and scribbles in his pad.

"You mention being short of money..."

I lean across and try to see his pad.

"If you've got a box for gambling, you can put a tick in it. A fucking big tick."

"On what?"

"Horses, football, boxing. Bookies not casinos. Got it from my old man, he loved the nags."

"How much?"

I stand slowly and empty my pockets onto Noel Kelly's desk. There's a lighter, two pound coins and two 20p's.

"I don't keep count, but I'm sure you can find out what I earn. Take off my rent, a bit for food, plus booze money. Anything left goes to Billy."

"Billy?"

"Billy Hill. Usually the one at the top of Beeston Hill. That's my favourite. They have comfy seats."

Noel Kelly falls silent as he scribbles his notes, and I watch his left foot tapping the floor as if there's a tune playing in his head.

"I think I know the next bit..."

He finishes his notes then looks up.

"The next bit?"

"Yeah, isn't it now that you tell me that my behavioural traits indicate a deep seated sense of self-loathing? That I punish myself through various forms of self-abuse because deep down I hate myself and have a subconscious urge to destroy myself, probably due to all the terrible things I've done in my life?"

Noel Kelly smiles.

"You after my job Charlie?"

"No, I couldn't keep it deadpan like you do. I'd tell people what pathetic wankers they really are."

A slight downward twitch of the eyebrow but he doesn't reply. He turns the page and taps his pen on the pad.

"You mentioned your brother. Drugs. Do you want to tell me about that?"

I look up at the artexed ceiling and take a deep breath, knowing I'm going to be diving too deep into that dark pool this time.

"Not really."

"If you don't feel like it that's fine..."

"I don't want to, but it's a big part of the story, so I will."

I stand and walk to the table by the window and pour myself a glass of water, speaking over the clink of ice cubes falling into the glass. Then I reach over to the Newton's Cradle and draw back one of the silver balls and release it, setting off the physics conundrum with its repetitive motion and metallic click-clack beat.

"After my mum and dad were killed, me and Andy went to live with our grandparents, my mother's mum and dad. Looking back, it must have been a nightmare for them. They'd have been in their early sixties then. Lose their daughter and get lumbered with two little lads. As you'd expect, we didn't make it easy for them. I was knocking off school most of the time, got brought home by the coppers a couple of times for nicking sweets and records from Woolworths. I was 14 or 15 when the 2-Tone thing kicked off in about '79."

I sit down and look at Noel Kelly perching on the edge of the seat in front of me. He looks like the sort of kid who would more likely listen to Pink Floyd or Hawkwind, so I think I'd better make sure he's keeping up.

"Do you remember 2 Tone Noel?"

"I was in my late twenties then, just married, but yeah I remember the Specials, Madness, the whole Mod revival thing."

As I thought, he's not really keeping up, and a lesson in street culture at the start of the eighties is required.

"That's how it was in the early days. Mods liked 2-Tone, you'd see kids with the checked patches on their parkas and they wore Harringtons in summer."

"Harringtons?" Noel Kelly was probably wearing patch covered denim at this point, but I wave my hand to dismiss his question.

"It was a jacket. Anyway by 1980 the scene had split, you were either a mod or a skinhead. Mods liked Secret Affair, the Jam and sixties stuff like the Who and Motown. Skinheads were into 2-Tone and early seventies reggae. You'd still play the other stuff in your bedroom, I loved the Jam, but you wouldn't admit it to your mates. By the middle of 1980, mods and skins were scrapping all the time."

"And which were you?"

I smile. "Skinhead was more my style. 18-eyelet docs, jeans up to my knees, yellow Harrington, Fred Perry, grade 1 on my head."

Noel Kelly is polishing his glasses on his sweater again and I realise that's his way of telling me he's about to speak.

"And your brother, Andy, he'd have been what, 12 or 13 then?"

He's good, telling me to get to the fucking point without me realising.

"Yeah, Andy was like my shadow. Never really had many mates of his own age, he was always hanging round with my gang. Always trying to impress us. You know the score – younger kid who was game for anything, never backing down, trying to show us how hard he was, justifying his place in the group I suppose."

Noel Kelly nods and scribbles in his pad and I pause, listening to the slowing click-clack rhythm of the desk toy until he looks up expectantly.

"Yeah...carry on when you're ready."

I'm staring at the glass of water in my hand and an image appears suddenly and unexpectedly in my mind. I'm standing in the doorway of the Black Lion. It's a sunny day, start of the football season. I'm wearing a Blue Fila BJ, bleached Levis' and Puma G Vilas trainers. I'm holding a bottle of Holsten Pils, scanning the corner and the road from the station, looking for Wolves or Everton or whoever we had that day. I look down towards Swinegate and see Andy approaching from under the railway bridge. He's wearing his knee length Docs and a black Fred Perry. He grins and waves as he sees me. He crosses the road in front of the Prince of Wales, rolling up the sleeve of his polo shirt to his shoulder to expose a gauze bandage covered in cellotape.

"Just been to Babs." Those were his words and my heart sank. The way he was at that time, I didn't want him to pull the plaster back. I didn't want to see what he'd had tattooed on his arm. I fucking lost it as soon as I saw the White Rose backed by a Union Jack and the words underneath. Yorkshire. National Front.

I can still see the hurt in his eyes as I grab hold of him by the collar, smash him into the pub door, tell him what a fucking idiot he is, that he's going to regret that for the rest of his life and that I'm done with him.

"You okay Charlie?" Noel Kelly's voice is soft, as if waking a sleeping child, and I look up from the glass of water.

"I abandoned him. Left my little brother and fucked off just when he needed me."

I can feel my heart pounding and I lift the glass and drain it in one gulp.

Noel Kelly raises a hand. "Okay...maybe take a step back. Was this the same time? 1980?"

"No this was a bit later. I'd grown out of the skinhead thing by the start of 81. I'd be 16 or 17 by now. Me and my mates could get served in pubs in town, the Gemini, Precinct, Jacomelli's sometimes. Andy was still a kid, he had no chance so he got pushed out of the group. Fashion had changed too, we grew our hair into a fringe, started wearing golf jumpers, decent jeans and trainers. We were going to Leeds games, twenty, thirty of us to start with, but it got bigger. We'd go on the normal train, the coppers would wave us past at the station and stop all the skinheads and scarfers. Then we'd pay in the seats where there was no segregation, and ...engage with like-minded kids from other teams. It was mental at times. I was scrapping more than when I was a skin."

"But Andy was still a skinhead?" Noel Kelly taps the end of his biro on his bearded chin.

"Yeah, and he was well into it by now. Tats all over his arms, fucking teardrop under his eye. And this is where it got really weird, I still can't really get my head round it. It had all started with 2 Tone, black and white unite and fight and all that, but as the number of skinheads declined, Andy started knocking about with some 'Oi' skins, lads who'd been punks, into Angelic Upstarts, Cockney Rejects, stuff like that."

Noel Kelly shakes his head and shrugs. I'm talking a foreign language to this university educated Irishman who had lived out his teenage years in rural Ireland amidst the prog-rock tedium of the early seventies.

"These lads were NF and British Movement. They used to meet at the Whip pub. Andy and his mates were still too young to get served, but they'd hang around in the yard outside. The older NF lads would buy them beer and get them to have a go at the students selling Socialist Worker on Briggate. They'd give them papers to sell. Flag, Bulldog, NF News, they used to flog them outside the Lowfields at Elland Road. I'd see Andy and his pals there, stood with all these older blokes. There was one in his late twenties, TC they called him, he was the leader, the organiser. Looked like Yozzer Hughes on Boys from the Blackstuff, big droopy tash and a gold hoop ear-ring. Jagged scar across his eye and down his cheek. I should have pulled the wanker then, asked what he was doing with a load of 15 year old kids. I should have stopped it all..."

I'm probably look for reassurance from Noel Kelly, vindication that I didn't abandon my kid brother when he needed me most, and I pause, awaiting his response. He shrugs.

"At that age, it's difficult. You were both trying to find your way in the world. You were a couple of years older than him, you were making that move into the adult world and for once, Andy couldn't follow you. He had to find his own path. At that age, your friends raise you as much as your family."

"But I wasn't there to show him the right path. I let him get lost." I stare at the empty glass that is shaking in my right hand. I realise I've paused again, probably waiting for Noel Kelly's reassurance which isn't going to come, so I carry on.

"I had my own problems at that time. As I said, I was into the football stuff. I'd had a couple of cautions, but then I got nicked at West Ham and it was serious. We'd come out of the tube station and came face to face with their lot. We were massively outnumbered, but back then we thought we were invincible. We might get done but we never run, that was our motto. We were in this street market and it was kicking off everywhere. Stalls getting tipped over, shoppers screaming, it was a proper riot." I catch myself smiling and so does Noel Kelly.

"It sounds like you were enjoying it. Slightly ironic given your current role."

"Yeah, I enjoyed it. We all did. West Ham had a big reputation then, they thought we'd back off, but we shocked them. Taught them a lesson in their own backyard. Unfortunately I got nicked. I'd picked up a sweeping brush and was swinging it at some of their lads. A copper came from behind and I span round and clumped him over the head with it."

"Ouch." Noel Kelly grimaces and the disapproving eye twitch returns.

"Exactly. I got done for Section 2 violent disorder and assault on a police officer. My solicitor said I was looking at 18 months."

"Given that you're now a serving police officer I'm guessing you somehow managed to avoid a custodial sentence?"

I nod and inhale then puff out my cheeks as I exhale. There's a shooting pain in my forehead and I wish I hadn't started telling the story.

"The brief told me there were only two sure-fire ways of avoiding getting sent down. One was to have a wife with a kid on the way. That wasn't going to happen with a court date in two months."

"What was the other?"

"Swap one sentence for another. Join the fucking army. I signed up for 4 years. I was 18. Got posted to Devizes in Wiltshire. It felt a long way away back then, and I didn't bother coming back up here much."

"And Andy? What was he doing at this point?"

I place the glass on the floor by my feet, close my eyes and anticipate the cold chill, as I plunge deeper into a dark pool of even darker memories.

"Andy was lost by that point. That path you mentioned, it took him to a bad place, a dark place he never came back from."

"What happened to him Charlie?"

I open my eyes and suddenly feel that I can't breathe, that I've gone too deep and I need to claw my way back towards the surface, back towards the light.

"Can we do this another time Noel? I think I'm done for today."

.

Chapter 13

I'm sitting in an unmarked car outside Nat West on Park Row. Eddie Young is in the driver's seat next to me and Pierre, the EGT photographer is in the backseat with a long lens trained on the door of the new Beckett's Bank pub across the road. It's midday, the golden hour for pre-match evidence capture, and I'm scanning the street and directing Pierre on which new arrivals are of interest.

"These four."

"Stevie Kenny in a nice new cream coloured CP Company jacket there, that'll stand out later." Eddie casts an eye on the lads as they pass us on their way from the Conservatory to the Wetherspoons pub which has taken over as the prime meeting place for our lads, since it opened at the start of the year.

"Nah, nothing happening today. No one wants to get nicked before the semi."

"You heard from Chelsea?"

I look at my phone. A missed call from Shivers but nothing from Bernie Maplin, Chelsea's FIO.

"Nothing since he rang to say they're in Wakey."

"Three buses is it?"

"It was an hour ago. I'm guessing they'll have picked up a few mini-buses since then. Most of their proper lot haven't bothered."

"How many bobbies are on the train?"

"Fuck me Eddie, what is it, twenty questions?"

I hear Pierre stifle a giggle in the back seat and Eddie Young flashes him a look in the mirror.

"Bernie's got a couple of spotters on the train, there's about a hundred on there, a few old lads, mainly drinkers though." I glance at my watch. "They should be just reaching Donny now. They're going to tell them to get off in Wakey or get wrapped up here. Up to them. I've made it clear I'm not having them wandering around town in small groups and I'm not sorting a fucking pub for them."

"These three Pierre." I nod out of the window and catch the eye of Craig Steel from Selby, who gives me a wave. I ignore him and watch them greet the bouncers at Becketts Bank, then I tug on the catch and push open the car door.

"Where you off to?"

I mutter 'for a walk' and slam the car door closed before Eddie Young hears me. I pull the Nokia from my jacket pocket and re-dial Shivers' number as I cross the road. He answers quickly and for once doesn't sound like he's in a pub.

"Where are you?" I pace outside the pub door, glancing down Greek Street towards All Bar One, where a gaggle of hens teeter on too-high-heels in the doorway.

"In a taxi to 'ground. Told you, we've got a box today."

"What did you want? All those names okay?"

"Yeah, yeah, perfect..." He pauses and through a hand over the phone I hear him say 'Charlie...the copper.'

Then he's back on full volume.

"Listen mate, he wants to see you."

"Who does?" I watch as a gang of lads walk past Nat West and flick a wanker sign at the camera in the backseat of our car.

"Danny."

They spot me outside the pub and a couple duck their heads and turn away. The others meet my stare as they cross the road and one draws the snot from his nose and expels it a couple of yards in front of me, then smiles and winks as he passes to enter the pub. I recognise him but don't know his name.

"Did you hear me mate?" I can hear a voice in the car with Shivers.

"Yeah, I heard you. What for?"

"I don't fucking know...he just wants to meet you, put a face to the name." I can hear the voice in the background, Danny Cade calling the shots again on his first full day out of the nick.

"Okay, East Stand is it? I'll see if I can get over at some point."

I hear Shivers say 'make sure...' as I kill the call and put the phone back in my jacket pocket. I nod to the bouncers and enter the pub. As its name suggests, Becketts Bank was once Barclays Bank, and its high ceilings are responsible for an acoustic sound effect which seems to amplify the human voice tenfold. The cumulative echo causes everyone to speak even louder in order to be heard, and anyone entering the pub is greeted by a deafening roar of conversation. Perhaps that's why no rival firms have ever attempted to 'take' the pub – any advance scouting party would reach the doorway and assume they were about to engage a mob of thousands.

I do the rounds, tolerating the usual ritual dance. I smile and name drop the 'Plod's Pals', watching them puff out their chests and take the piss behind my back, enjoying the kudos of being 'known risk'; I clock the hostiles, looking them up and down, taking note of what they're wearing, smirking at some hideous Paul & Shark cardigan that Ted Heath would have binned in 1973; I exchange some banter with the drinkers, the straight members in their Strongbow shirts and club anoraks. A decent turn-out as you'd expect, but the atmosphere is muted, lacking the undercurrent of a game when you know it's likely to go off. Man Utd obviously, or someone who's rumoured to be bringing a bus and landing somewhere clever, Spurs or maybe someone a bit under-rated but with potential on the right day like Boro or Birmingham. Chelsea should be a big one, but they've done nothing up here in twenty years and no one expects much today.

I exit out of the other door and make my way down to the car, giving Bernie Maplin a call as I walk.

"How's it going down there?"

Maplin is Glaswegian west end and I struggle to understand one word in four, but I manage to deduce that they have three busloads wrapped up in two pubs and another eighty coming off the train. The plan is to load them back on their buses and put a double decker on for the train lot, then bring them all in together at 2pm.

"None of mine turned up then?"

"Aye, there's about forty plotted up in the Elephant and Castle. Canine units on the doors, they're going nowhere."

"They won't be trying to. Most of them are banned or not bothered. They have to turn up though, it's their town, can't have you cockney cunts drinking in it unopposed..."

"First time I've been called that!" Bernie Maplin laughs and kills the call and we arrange to meet at the Bremner statue at 2.30.

"Where to? Check out Mill Hill?" Eddie Young turns the key in the ignition as I climb into the passenger seat.

"Yeah, wherever you think." Normally I'd be telling him there'll be no faces in Spencers yet, that it's worth checking out Bar Censsa on Boar Lane on the way down, or even Break for the Border where a few lads have started to go after the game. Normally, but not today. Today I'm not thinking of Cat C's and backstreet battles, today my mind is racing, full of thoughts of Danny fucking Cade.

Chapter 14

It had started in the usual way. Some cockney teenager, pumped up on strong Wakey lager and a gram of Colombia's finest, getting into it with the staff on the South Stand concourse over an ice-filled pie or the wrong change or a stupid accent. Then in come the stewards, minimum wage imports from Zimbabwe, full of their own importance in their high-vis jackets and lanyards. Given some authority for the first time in their miserable lives and guaranteed to overstep the mark. Pushing and shoving turning to wrestling and fists, then our lads piling in with batons drawn and before you know it, we've got a situation. Twenty law facing off against fifty Chelsea and word spreading up in the seats, attracting their hostiles down to test the mettle of the WYP firm.

I stand to the side and direct EGT Pierre on where to point his lens as Eddie Young, eyes flashing with excitement, stands on the frontline alongside seen-it-all-before Bernie Maplin. I duck as a half-filled plastic pint glass arcs above my head and bounces off a stanchion, showering us all in tepid lager or lukewarm piss, take your pick.

The opposite side aren't going anywhere, mobbed up by the bar, now numbering seventy or eighty, arms extended, the concourse echoing to their chanting. 'Chelsea...Chelsea...Chelsea.' My radio crackles and I step back and press it to my ear.

"PC Mills...PC Mills, are you there Charlie? Over."

I have to shout to make myself heard.

"Yes control, I'm here. Over."

"Message from Silver Commander. Please call him immediately."

If Tony Hudson knew how hard it was to get a mobile phone signal under the South Stand during a match, he could have got in his fucking car and driven here from Holbeck quicker than I'll be able to call him.

"Message received control. Will try and make contact but mobile phone signal isn't good. Can't he come to the control room? Over."

The radio crackles as control seem to be interpreting my 'fuck you' response.

"Negative, PC Mills. Silver Commander made clear that communication must be on a secure line. Over."

Fucks sake. I catch Eddie Young's eye and point at my radio and shake my head, then turn and head up the slope leading from the South Stand to the turnstiles on Elland Road. I locate a Zimbabwean key holder and cross the road, past the newsagent, and stride up Heath Grove, mobile phone in hand. Turn left then carry on towards the top of the cul-de-sac of Heath Rise. As I reach the two semis at the top of the street, I spot a fat man in a dust covered overall standing beside a skip, talking into a mobile phone. I stop and lean on the wall of number 23, flicking through the address book until I reach 'T' and the entry for 'Teeth Tony'.' I select the name and press the green button on the Nokia.

Tony Hudson surprises me by answering after a single ring.

"Mills? Is that you?"

"Yes sir. Couldn't get a signal in the ground."

"Never mind. Can you hear me? What I'm about to tell you is very, very important." His tone is one of agitated excitement and I can imagine his tiny teeth flashing behind spittle coated lips as he speaks.

"Yes, I can hear you."

"Do you know Danny Cade?"

Danny Cade. The two words land like an explosion in my head and I rock backwards against the wall.

"Danny Cade..." I'm back in the water again, watching the daylight disappear above me, gasping for breath.

"Danny Cade is the leader of a North Leeds OCG. He was jailed six years ago for aiding an offender. That offender was an associate called Ryan Green who is serving twenty years for attempted murder and possession of a firearm. This morning Ryan Green was taken from HMP Leyland by ambulance after complaining of chest pains. The ambulance transporting him was rammed by a vehicle on the outskirts of Chorley. The two HMP officers accompanying Green were shot. One is in a critical condition...Can you still hear me Mills?"

I can just about hear him, but his voice is becoming muffled as I sink down into the dark pool. I rest on the garden wall and feel myself plunging deeper and deeper, the light above me now almost gone.

"I'm here sir yes." I manage to whisper.

"Danny Cade was released from prison this week, and is currently in the Elland Road stadium in a Corporate hospitality box with a number of key associates. Officers from Millgarth OCU are about to execute an operation to bring Cade and others in for questioning. An armed response team will be arriving outside the stadium shortly. They will undertake the apprehension of the suspects fifteen minutes after play has resumed for the second half. I need you to meet DCI Harker of OCU outside the stadium and explain the layout of the Corporate Hospitality area, and provide the location of the box Cade is occupying. I also need you to speak to stadium management and get them to clear the area of all their employees and arrange evacuation of the two adjoining corporate hospitality boxes using the pretext of a fire alarm. I need you to do this immediately PC Mills. Do you understand?"

What I understand is that Shivers is in that box. Shivers phone has my contact details, and the call history shows how many times I've spoken to him today and over the last few weeks.

I'm already running down Heath Rise gasping for breath.

"I understand sir. On it now."

Chapter 15

I'm unsure whether anyone has ever doubled over and vomited onto the club crest carpet within seconds of passing through the double glass doors of the Elland Road east stand. I'm pretty certain no serving police officer had ever done that, until I stumbled down the stairs, sweating and purple faced, then became reacquainted with my pre-match burger in front of the horrified receptionist in her smart blue club blazer.

"Get Ian Hegarty here now! Tell him I need to speak to him urgently." I gasp at the wide-eyed blonde woman as I wipe the puke from my chin then push past her and head towards the stairs.

I'd tried calling Shivers as I ran back down towards the ground, but by the time I reached Heath Grove I couldn't even get the posh woman's voice telling me the mobile phone I was calling may be switched off. There was only one thing for it, I'd have to try and get to him in person, and hope that no one noticed that the corporate box being raided at 4.15 had been visited by Leeds United's FIO just half an hour earlier.

Luckily the boxes all have a glass door opening onto a corridor so I'm able to assess the occupants as I pass. Half a dozen disinterested middle aged women getting pissed on white wine while their husbands watch the match from the balcony; A gang of silver-haired men in golf jumpers, standing terrace style, pints in hand, watching through the window; John Mclelland holding court, a group of thirty-somethings more interested in his tales than the game. Then.. a dozen shaven heads. Tattoos. Stone Island and CP Company. A table full of bottles, packets of powder, a cloud of weed smoke on the balcony. I tap on the glass door and Husky from

Whitkirk turns and raises his eyebrows. I point to Shivers and Husky's lips move and Shivers swivels and our eyes meet. His are laughing, pissed, excited. Mine are wide in panic. He pushes his way to the back of the box and opens the door.

"Alright mate. Glad you made it, come in. Danny's outside on the balcony."

I grab hold of his jacket and shake him.

"Shivers, listen to me. You're about to get raided. You're all going to get nicked, and they'll find your phone with my number. We're fucked Shivers. You have to get out of here now!"

I still have hold of Shivers' jacket and am staring into his red eyes. I don't know why I have hold of him, maybe I expect him to collapse in shock or try to bolt or something. But he doesn't. He smiles. He nods his head. Then he starts laughing.

"You heard then? About Ryan?"

I stare back at him, my mind struggling to comprehend his reaction.

"Great news innit? Perfect timing while we're all here for three hours with thirty five thousand witnesses."

"But Millgarth OCU are going to nick you all. They're on the way now..."

"What can they do? They can't link us to it, and clearly we weren't there, because we're all here. And it's a shit game anyway, I'll be glad to get out."

"What about your phone?"

"All gone. Harehills Macca wasn't bothered for the match, he's more of a Rangers fan, so he fucked off with everyone's mobiles before kick-off. Don't worry Millsy, it's all good. Nothing to link us to you, and young Ryan is somewhere safe and he's 100% ready to get back to work. He's about to start marking your homework mate!"

Chapter 16

I wake in a panic, thinking I had to be back on shift but then I remember my session with Noel. The sun is shining on the river when I lift the roller blind overlooking the cobbled car park of my flat in Navigation Walk, and I decide a walk might clear my head. I recoil after sniffing a carton of milk, the only item in the fridge, and contemplate the remnants of a two litre bottle of Frosty Jack which stands amidst the detritus on the kitchen worktop. I pour half a glass, and swill it and sniff it and raise it to my lips, but it looks like piss and I can't be sure it isn't, so I tip it down the sink and pour myself a pint of water, then another.

Out of the flat, along the cobbles to Dock Street and the Adelphi. Right, over Leeds Bridge, pausing to hawk up a couple of lungfuls of mucous that look and taste like tar. I glance up Lower Briggate and see the old tailor rattling the grill open at Class Fashions, just as he has every day for the last thirty years. I turn left along Swinegate, past the old City Tramways headquarters, now turned into what they call a boutique hotel. Past the wasteland that used to be the Queens Hall, a grand title for a tram storage shed, but that was enough to pull in plenty of musical big hitters over the years. Up under the railway bridge towards Mill Hill, a street full of memories, and I feel my heart rate suddenly quicken and struggle to catch my breath. I'm wondering why I came this way. My hands are soaked in sweat as I reach the corner and look across from the Prince of Wales towards Spencers, once the Black Lion. I close my eyes and breathe in through my nose for a count of four. Hold for six. Exhale for four. I feel my breathing begin to slow as I imagine immersing myself in the cold, dark water and I try to forget about

Andy with his new tattoo, pinned to the wall in the pub doorway.

Up past Mill Hill amusements, dodging a team of carpet cleaners lugging equipment into Bar Censsa, once the reception area of the Griffin Hotel. I glance over Boar Lane at the shiny façade of Leeds Shopping Plaza, a new development to replace the Bond Street Centre. The iconic orange tube of its escalator entrance now gone, and a huge Mothercare store in place of Jacomellis. The irony of the Very Young Team being replaced by an even younger one. I walk slowly up Park Row, past Becketts Bank with Shivers' words echoing in my head. 'He's ready to start work...marking your homework.' Ryan Green, Danny Cade's top triggerman, back on the streets with a shopping list in his pocket. A shopping list I've written. A tide of nausea rises in my stomach, and I have to swallow hard to stop myself puking outside the steps of the Bank, now reinvented as O'Neill's Bar.

Up Cookridge Street, past the old Leeds Permanent building, soon to reopen as a four star hotel, and yet another upmarket shopping mall with an aspirational name, this one destined to be called 'The Light.' The old city changing before my eyes, like a snake shedding its skin. Dirty Leeds, the motorway city, turning itself into skyscraper city, shopping centre city. Like a 1940's whore perched on a bar stool in the Robin Hood on Vicar Lane, flicking her painted eyelashes at a yank serviceman, Leeds is now hitching up its skirt and bending over to attract southern money, foreign money.

I feel the first spots of rain as a boat appears on the horizon and I make a quick right, past the Rat and Parrot and over the road into Morrisons, where I buy three cans of Red Bull. Then out and up past the Pig and Whistle, now boarded up, no doubt awaiting its rebirth as yet another café bar. Past the Cobourg, still hanging on as a pub for now, on towards the old coal barge marooned on a traffic island opposite the Poly, that is the Dry Dock. By the time I pass the University, I've downed all the Red Bull and the rain is slanting into my face like the spray of a watering can, and thoughts of Ryan Green and the names on that list are racing through my brain like an electric shock. I push the thoughts away. Fuck them, none of them are civilians. Live by the sword, die by the sword.

Whoever named Woodhouse Moor clearly had a sense of humour. Rather than the rolling acres of heather the word conjures up, the Leeds 6 version is a flat expanse of windswept, muddy, ash fragments that becomes a puddled quagmire in wet weather. With my head down, walking into the driving rain, I'm forced to stare at my feet and I curse at the purple brown mud that has now coated my new Stan Smiths. The rain seeps through my coat and my sweatshirt and trickles down my spine and I can now feel it soaking the arse of my jeans and my boxer shorts.

By the time I ring Noel's bell, I'm on no mood to spend another hour talking about a fucked up life, but I am ready for a cup of hot tea.

Chapter 17

"My God Charlie, you're soaking wet. What happened? Are you okay?"

Noel Kelly's normally unruffled demeanour slips as he opens his office door and looks me up and down.

"Tough couple of days Noel." I shuffle into the room and unzip my sodden jacket and let it fall to the floor.

"Let me get you a drink to warm you up. Here, take off those wet clothes." I half smile as Kelly morphs into my grandfather again, fussing around me after I'd been pushed into the canal at Kirkstall by James Fogarty when I was eleven.

"Tell me what's been going on then..."

I pull a soaked sweatshirt over my head and sit down, contemplating what to tell him about the last few days.

I'd kept my head down at the ground when Millgarth Organised Crime Unit had spoilt Danny Cade's coming home party. Not that it had seemed to bother Cade and his lads, who'd even tried to finish their pints at gunpoint, before being marched down to the vans waiting to transport them to Millgarth. Everyone at OCU had gone dark after the game, and no one at Holbeck knew anything, only that one of the screws had undergone surgery to remove shotgun pellets from his stomach and was expected to survive. I'd checked the message boards, then knocked off at nine and gone for a few pints in town. Square on the Lane, the Hogshead, then down to Cuban Heels behind the Corn Exchange. I was up early on the Sunday, in the office for ten, checking the message boards again. A bit on ITK from Chelsea about the incident in the South Stand, and a couple of questions on the Service Crew board about the police activity in the East Stand, but OCU seemed to have done a good job in keeping the op pretty low key. The office was quiet, so there was none of the usual chatter picked up on the grapevine from Millgarth, and there were no charges showing on PNC against Cade or Shivers or any of the other lads, so I'd guessed they'd all been released.

They say God gives with one hand and takes with the other and that proved unfortunately accurate with Saturday's correct score treble giving me a 280 quid return on a ten quid bet, then a ten year old Ford Orion which sputtered and ground to a halt in Rowland Road as I'd set off to Beeston William Hills to collect my winnings. Dark clouds were looking ominous as I'd walked along Lodge Lane, a steady drizzle was falling as I turned the corner into Beeston Road, and I was piss-wet through by the time I shoved open the door into the familiar fug of smoke and damp anoraks at Hills. I'd sorted my bets for the day, but it was still raining as I emerged onto the street with a spring in my step and ten twenties in my pocket, so I'd headed straight over to the White Hart for a livener. I've no idea what time I left but I can vaguely remember watching Celtic beat Rangers, and it being dusk when I got outside. I was another sixty quid down, which told me I'd probably got a taxi home, and the taste in my mouth and the red stains on my polo shirt informed my copper's intuition that I'd got the driver to stop for a kebab somewhere.

So that was my last few days, and I look across at Noel, unfolding his pad and looking for a pen, and I contemplate what to say. I lean forward and ruffle my hair, watching the rain droplets splash and settle on the laminate floor. Noel crosses his legs in the seat opposite me and taps his pen on his pad.

"Just work stuff really, you know, nothing of interest."

Noel Kelly smiles and nods, then flicks a page in his pad and runs his finger along the hand written notes.

"So, last time, we were talking about Andy, your brother. You started to tell me what happened with him and how you feel about that?"

I take a deep breath, in for four, hold for six, then exhale slowly, preparing to go under again, to plumb the depths, lose sight of the light of the surface.

"You told me that Andy had fallen in with a right wing crowd, that maybe you felt he was being manipulated by some older guys..."

I pause and close my eyes, feeling my breath slowing, my heartbeat decreasing as I imagine sinking down into the darkness.

"Yeah...So Andy was well into the whole skinhead NF thing by now. This would have been early '82 I guess. He was hanging around the Starlight Room amusements on Lower Briggate, playing the space invaders and the bandits. He was still at school and was basically an errand boy for the older NF blokes who drank in the Whip. The bloke I told you about, TC, the Yozzer Hughes lookalike, he was running things around town. The young lads were like his foot soldiers. I knew of him because there was a crossover between the NF and some of the football lads, but I just thought he was a scruffy wanker, not worth bothering about. So, I knew all this stuff was happening and Andy was involved, but I had my court case, then before I knew it, I'd signed up and was being shipped down to Wiltshire for basic training. The truth is, I just didn't have time for Andy."

"As we discussed last time, that's totally understandable. You were a young man, facing your own issues, trying to make your way in the world. You couldn't be expected to act as a parent to a troubled teenager too." Noel Kelly speaks softly and quietly. He's good, he knows he's getting close now, within touching distance.

"Yeah, so I was down South, I only really heard second hand from my grandma what happened."

"And what did happen?"

I close my eyes, feel the cold water surrounding me, feel myself sinking down deeper into the darkness, the light of the sky hard to see now.

"There was a concert in Potternewton Park, Rock Against Racism."

"Yeah, I remember Rock against Racism. It was a big thing in the late seventies." Noel Kelly is eager to show he was once down with the kids.

"Probably, yeah, so the Specials were playing at Potty Park, and a few reggae bands. There was going to be a march from Woodhouse Moor, through town and up to the park. Obviously the NF lads couldn't stand for that in their town, so the plan was to attack the march as it went along Regent Street, past the car showrooms. Of course, it wouldn't be TC and the older lads getting their hands dirty. It was going to be Andy and his mates. Kids of fifteen, sixteen, I think the oldest was seventeen."

Noel opens his mouth to speak but doesn't, and nods for me to continue.

"Thankfully, it never happened. Someone got nicked the week before the gig and grassed them up, so the coppers knew it was going to happen. As us coppers do though, we let it go ahead, up to a point."

"So what happened?"

"Andy and three other lads had a milk crate filled with twelve petrol bombs in a van parked in Byron Street. None of them even had a licence, but no one seemed interested in how they'd managed to get hold of this old van with no plates."

"Acquired by the older National Front leaders no doubt."

"Of course, that was obvious. Anyway, they were parked up waiting, milk crate in the back, balaclavas on, as the march was passing the Playhouse. That's when the police stepped in. Nicked all four of them. He got five years youth custody."

Noel Kelly sighs and begins writing in his pad then stops and looks at me.

"I can see why you think you failed him Charlie, but in reality, even if you'd been in Leeds, there's a good chance he would have made those wrong choices anyway.

"Maybe. We'll never know though because I wasn't."

Only the ticking of the clock breaks the silence, and I feel the familiar tightness in my chest, my breathing becoming quicker.

"I get the feeling that's not the end...?"

My heart is beating faster now, and I have to focus on slowing my breathing. Prepare myself to sink even deeper, away from the sky, to a place of total darkness.

"He was in Kirklevington Detention Centre, up near Middlesbrough. I knew he was in there, he'd been in about nine months, but I never went to see him. Told my gran I couldn't get enough time off to travel back North. The truth was, I didn't want to see him in there. I was scared of seeing him, scared of what he'd become. So again, I only know what I've been told. That he was getting bullied, maybe because of the NF tats, I don't know. I heard that he got into smack, smoking it not shooting up as far as I know. Then..."

I pause and Noel Kelly looks up from his pad, knowing what's coming.

"Then they found him in his room. He'd hung himself off the frame of a bunk bed with a belt."

I hear Noel exhale through his nose like he's deflating.

"How old was he?"

"Sixteen....just sixteen. What a fucking waste eh?"

Noel Kelly nods and sinks lower into his comfy seat, his pen resting on the pad. I know I shouldn't, but I can't resist, and he looks at me like he's expecting it.

"Remember what you said one of the first times we met Noel?"

He closes his eyes and nods his head slowly.

"You still think I'm lucky then?"

Chapter 18

Sometimes, when there's something big happening, you can feel it as soon as you walk through the doors of the nick. An electricity, a buzz. The way people are moving, with an urgency and a purpose. The snatched conversations on the stairs, in the yard, at the counter in the canteen. It's days like this that make the humdrum tedium of what's really a glorified office job worthwhile. Today there are two names on everyone's lips – Ryan Green and Danny Cade.

"He was seen in 'lift at Lovell Park Towers. They reckon he's taken over 'flats on 'top floor. It'll be a chopper job with armed forces support, you watch."

Eddie Young is holding court, sitting on his desk, addressing a couple of specials and Helen with the ginger hair.

"He's quite fit Cade, isn't he?" She's leaning over to see an old mugshot of Danny on a computer monitor.

"You wouldn't mind a one-on-one interrogation with him cuffed to the chair then Hel?" Young nods over to me as I sit down and turn on the computer, listening to the clicks and whirrs as it slowly comes to life.

"Body builder apparently. Bulked up in 'nick."

"Nah, he was always into all that." I say it almost to myself without thinking and immediately regret it as the four of them all turn to face me.

"You had dealings with him then Charlie?"

I'm backpedalling now. "No, he went to my school though. Couple of years younger than me. My brother knew him better than I did."

"You've heard about this morning then?" Young is looking at me in that way he does when he knows something I don't.

"No what's happened?"

"Body in a car boot at Golden Acre park. A bullet through each eye socket is what they're saying."

I feel my heart pounding and my palms are suddenly sweating as I tap the keyboard on the desk. It's started then. Ryan's gone shopping.

"They think it's Cade then?" I try to sound unconcerned and probably fail.

"Who else is it going to be? He only got out a few days ago. Sprung his top trigger man straight away, it's obvious isn't it?"

"What is?"

The screen lights up with the blue crest of WYP and I don't look at Young, who's now stood up from the desk and has walked to the window, looking out at the graffiti scarred gable end of Primrose Lane as he delivers his expert judgement.

"The King is back to reclaim his throne. There's going to be a war on the streets boys and girls. And I can't fucking wait!"

Chapter 19

' The Stuff Dreams are Made Of '- Leeds United Stand on the brink of the biggest achievement in their recent history. Paul Robinson looks back over the club's unlikely rise to the pinnacle of European football. A football article on Page 7 of the YEP highlights the importance of Wednesday's semi-final.

I turn the back page to read Phil Rostron describing Leeds as the 'It' team of British football, poised to send shock waves through the Premier League by landing Spurs captain Sol Campbell in a sensational summer transfer swoop. I take a swig of my pint and gaze out of the window at Sparrow's Wharf bar onto the slow flowing grey river below. I then force myself to turn the paper over and look again at the face staring back at me from the front page.

Dark eyes underlined by sleep deprived shadows stare back at me, above a hooked Pashtun nose and thin lips downturned in a mugshot sneer. Malik Ishmael, 24. The body in the boot. Top of the shopping list. Missing eyeballs suggesting he'd obviously seen too much.

I stare back out of the window and try to ignore a rising feeling of nausea in the pit of my stomach. I catch the echoes of conversation from three men in suits standing at the bar. Apart from them and me and a teenage barmaid, the pub is weekday afternoon empty. It's the closest place to my flat, but I rarely come here. The red brickwork and bare floorboards make it feel too much like you're drinking in the cellar of the old warehouse it once was. 'Don't shit on your own doorstep'. That was one of my grandad's sayings and I'm now regretting agreeing to Shivers' suggestion that we meet here. 'Has to be somewhere quiet, out of the way where no one will know you or Danny. And no fucking Elvis.'

I pick up the YEP and fold it into my jacket pocket as I see them coming down the steps. Shivers leading the way, Mille Miglia viewshield jacket zipped right up under his chin and an Aquascutum baseball cap pulled low over his eyes. Behind him, the man himself. Daniel Liam Cade. Scanning the room as he enters, guard up, the gait of a man who's spent the last 6 years inside. He looks just how I remember him. Wide face with a Desperate Dan jawline and dark hair with a tendency to curl if grown too long. A grey hoody, stone washed jeans and big white Nikes. Cade was never into the dresser look.

Shivers spots me as they head to the bar, waggling his hand in a drinking gesture to ask if I want another. I stick up a thumb and drain off the three quarter pint I have left. I stare out of the window, watching their reflection in the glass, trying to slow my breathing. My palms are sweating so much I can barely hold my glass.

"Keeping it old school then Shivers?" I nod at the cap as he sits down and he takes it off, smiling. Danny Cade remains standing, and I can feel his eyes on me, assessing me, scoping out this bent pig on his payroll.

"Danny, this is Charlie."

I wipe my palms on my jeans under the table but they're already soaked again by the time I stand up to take hold of Danny Cade's extended hand.

"I remember you." He looks me in the eye and a semblance of a smile plays on his lips. "Allerton Grange."

"Yeah, I was a couple of years above you I think. You might have been in our kid's year. Andy...Andy Mills?"

The faint smile disappears but he doesn't blink. Shakes his head. 'No, don't remember him."

Cade sits down and stirs his half pint of coke with a straw, making the ice cubes clink.

Shivers breaks the silence before any of us have chance to notice it.

"So, Danny wanted to meet you Charlie, put a face to the name..."

"I want to know if I can trust you." Danny Cade sucks on the straw and narrows his eyes as the cold drink reaches his mouth, but doesn't shift his stare from my face.

"I've given you the names you wanted."

"Why though?" Cade lowers the glass and tilts his head back as he looks at me.

"I need the money. I'm fucking skint to be honest, simple as that."

"Why? You've got a job. Copper's pay isn't bad with the overtime."

I can sense Shivers shuffling in his seat next to me.

"I've got a daughter I have to pay for...I'm also a bit too partial to a flutter. And this." I lift my glass and take a swig.

"You used to work in London?"

"Yeah, I came out of the army and joined the Met."

"Doing what?" Danny Cade is biting his lip and his nostrils are flaring slightly. Never good signs in an interview and it now feels like this is turning into one.

"Standard plod stuff. Paddington, Tottenham, a bit south of the river, Brixton, Croydon.""

He nods. "So how've you ended up back here?"

I shrug. "Opportunity. I fancied the football job and they liked me in the interview. The fact that I'm from here and was involved in it all as a kid seemed to impress them."

Shivers lights a cigarette and blows smoke across the table causing Danny Cade to grimace and wave his hand.

"Involved as a kid? He's still involved now. Always makes sure we know what's what does Charlie."

Danny Cade grunts and nods slowly, then for the first time, shifts his attention from me and looks out of the window to the River Aire and the new developments springing up on the south bank.

"When we were kids, this was all derelict. Warehouses, disused factories, wasteland used for car parking. Remember that?"

I nod but he isn't looking.

"All this part of town was dead, decaying, like it was just waiting for the river to wash it all away. Look at it now...new bridges, hotels, bars, night clubs. The Royal Armouries moving up here, this new Light Shopping Centre on the Headrow. Why do you think that's all happened?"

"Someone saw the potential. Big city, people moving up from London to work in the new NHS building, cash coming in. Makes sense."

Danny Cade looks back at me and picks up his glass of coke.

"That's all true, but it's more than that. It needed someone with a big idea. A big idea and the fucking bollocks to make it all happen." He leans across the table and smiles and I can smell his aftershave. He sucks on the straw and licks his lips.

"I've just done six years, right? You probably think, what a waste of a life. Six years banged up, doing fuck all but lifting weights for half an hour a day and talking shite with whatever crackhead you're padded up with?"

It seems he wants an answer but neither agreeing or disagreeing seem a good option, so I keep quiet and take a swig of my beer until he starts talking again.

"And you'd be right to think that Charlie. It would be a waste, if all I did was lift some weights and talk shite with druggies. But that's not what I did. Do you want to know what I spent my time doing?"

I'm guessing it wasn't a flower arranging course or building York Minster out of matchsticks, and I nod as enthusiastically as I can.

"I spent my time making connections. Building networks. Listening and learning. I made sure I was kept in Top Security nicks, no cat D. That's why I served the full term. If I thought I was in danger of getting shifted down, I'd chin some cunt during association. Maybe threaten a screw, say I knew where his missus worked, that type of shit. Do you know why I did that Charlie?" He looks over his shoulder at the men in suits talking loudly as they leave. Just us now.

"I wanted to spend my time in Max Security so I could meet the right people. The proper lads. Blokes who've made the jump from running small operations in their own areas to controlling national networks with international links. I wanted to meet them, learn from them. I want to fucking be them." Danny Cade slams his glass down on the table and folds his arms as he gauges my response.

"Makes sense. As you said, it just needs someone to see the potential, and have an idea." I try to maintain eye contact but feel his stare is burning into my brain, reading my thoughts.

"So where does that leave us? Where do you fit in? If I were you, that's the question I'd be asking."

Shivers puts his cigarette out in an ash tray on the table and Danny Cade hands him his empty glass without looking at him. Shivers stands and turns to me.

"Another Charlie...? Course you fucking do."

Danny Cade waits until he heads to the bar before continuing.

"So Charlie, there are two phases to this plan. Phase one, clear the decks in Leeds. Get rid of all the little wannabe gangsters and bit-part players who've been squabbling over scraps while I've been away. That's happening now. The hard part was tracking these fuckers down, as they tend to keep moving around. The info you've provided is going to make that happen, and once the first few start to go down, the fear will spread through the rest like a fucking contagion." He looks over his shoulder towards Shivers chatting up the girl behind the bar.

"Then Phase two. Phase two is where we step it up a gear. Phase two is where we become those proper lads I talked about. Where we go national, then international." His eyes flash with excitement and he glances over his shoulder to see Shivers heading back towards us, laughing, with two pints and a coke in his hands.

"Phase two is the big move, Charlie. Proper money, serious money. You can add a couple of noughts onto what I've been paying you, because for this phase Charlie, I'm going to need your help."

Chapter 20

The Orion is running again, that's the good news, I tell myself as I pull up outside the row of Edwardian terraces in Hyde Park.

I don't need to glance at the YEP resting on the passenger seat to remind myself of the bad news. It was the second item on the Aire FM bulletin, after Nelson Mandela and Lucas Radebe opening the new square in front of the Civic Hall. It was on Calendar and Look North last night. It's the subject of every WYP special briefing that's been issued over the last two days. Gang Warfare they're calling it. Another body in another boot. Tropical World car park at Roundhay this time. No face left and no name yet, but I know for a fact that it will be one that I know. One that I've scribbled down an address for, then handed over in a pub.

The same as the lad shot outside Killingbeck Asda in front of his wife and kids by a masked man on a motorbike. Millgarth are still sitting on the detail, but I'm guessing he was one of a couple of LS9 names on the list. The bouncer blasted with a sawn-off in the Chained Bull doorway in a drive-by shooting is an easier one. Kelvin Browne. PNC only had an old address but it did have a current workplace. Easy pickings for Ryan Green, making good progress on marking my homework.

Noel Kelly opens the door with his customary smile and a half joke about an improvement in the weather from last time.

I sit down and we exchange pleasantries.

"How's things?"

Well Noel, I've illegally accessed confidential police data and provided details to a dangerous fugitive who is now laying waste to Leeds' criminal landscape, and I'm an integral part of phase 2 of an OCG boss's plan to take over the world. So things are going pretty fucking well I'd say.

"Yeah fine, usual stuff, you know."

Noel nods and opens his pad, running his finger along his old notes as if he's forgotten all about my brother topping himself in borstal aged 16.

"So, we've talked about your parents and your brother and what happened to them and how that's affected you. We've also touched on the death of your partner..."

"Keeley. Her name was Keeley."

I save Noel the trouble of flicking back in his pad.

"Keeley, yes, her death and the impact that had on you professionally and also in your personal life. You've spoken about your work in SCD10, the strain of deep undercover operations. I'd like us to talk through that a bit more if that's okay?"

I shrug. "Whatever you think."

"I'd like to go back to when you left the army and joined the police. Why you made the decisions you did at that time?"

I stand and walk over to the small table by the window, pour myself a glass of water, peer through the curtains at a squirrel hopping across the scrubby grass of the lawn, then turn to face Noel, sitting facing my empty chair.

"1988. I was 23. I'd done five years in the army and wanted out. After what had happened with Andy, I wanted to come back up North. Obviously, looking back, I felt guilty. My grandad had died by then and my gran wasn't well, but Gemma was a southern lass, she didn't fancy Yorkshire. I had a mate who'd left the forces the year before and joined the Met. They had a fast-track recruitment scheme for ex-services personnel. Basically, if you could walk in a straight line and had a basic command of English you were in. So we moved to London and I became a PC in the Met. Tottenham at first, it wasn't long after Broadwater Farm and Blakelock so that was interesting. I worked with a lot of seriously fucked up lads, but it was an education."

I walk back across the room, pausing to set the Newton's Cradle in motion and smile at the downward twitch of Noel's eyebrow as the staccato click-clack rhythm clashes with the ticking of the clock.

"But that wasn't undercover work, I'm guessing?"

"No this was basic plod stuff. The undercover job came about by accident. I had this shitty old Escort, T Reg, 1979. This would have been early 90's. Anyway, it needed a new exhaust to get through the MOT and, as usual, I was skint. A lad in the pub told me about a place that did cheap parts south of the river at Vauxhall, so I went down straight after a nightshift. Typical sketch, proper south London cliché - under the railway arches, cobbles, scrapyards, dogs on chains, you get the picture. I was there just after six in the morning and obviously they weren't open yet, so I pushed the seat back and went to sleep for an hour. I woke up as they were pulling the shutters open at the unit next door and popped my head up above the dashboard. There were two cars parked outside, a Cavalier and a VW Golf GTI, both pretty new, but it was the lads driving them that caught my eye. Kids off my patch, proper wrong 'uns that I knew well. I ducked my head down again and waited. The two motors disappeared inside the unit and I decided to hang around a bit. I was there four hours that morning and I saw half a dozen cars arrive, all driven by lads I knew had form. Next morning, I was back at six again, making notes of number plates, names, I even borrowed my mate's camera to try and get some photos."

Noel smiles and his blue eyes flash, reminding me of my grandad again.

"Did you get any evidence?"

"No, the cameras back then were pretty shit, but I went and told my gaffer, then I got pulled in by CID. They'd had word there was a big ringing operation and chop shop paying good money to young twoc'ers, but they hadn't been able to trace it. They were well pleased with what I'd found, and I got seconded to CID for six weeks as a Level 2 operative. We took the operation down and the blokes running it got some decent jail time. My gaffers seemed to like me and told me there was an opening, so to cut a long story short, I did all the courses and eventually became a UC officer, worked my way up and ended up in SCD10.

Noel is scribbling in his pad.

"Right, so you almost fell into undercover work by accident, but you found you were good at it, maybe that you enjoyed it?"

I pause and think back to the mid 90's and my role as a Level 2 operative. Posing as a smackhead and making test purchases from street dealers, sometimes helping Level 1 UC's create their legends. It was easy work for me. For the first time in my life, it had felt like I was actually doing something worthwhile and there was an element of excitement, without any real danger. I went home after my shift, earned decent money and slept well every night. Only I had to take it to the next fucking level, like I always do.

"Was it maybe that you liked the danger, that feeling of living on the edge?"

I nod but I'm not really listening. The words of my old mentor, Lenny Kabinski, my first boss at SCD10, are playing on a loop in my head and I smile.

"What is it?" Noel notices as he looks up from his pad.

"Something my old gaffer used to say. It's the best description of undercover work I've ever heard. The best description of my life.. of me."

"Go on..." Noel taps his pen on the pad.

"Lenny used to say that as an undercover officer you have to be prepared to swim in a big, dark pool of filth. To dive down and immerse yourself in it. To sink so low that it seeps into your pores. So it fills your mouth and nose so you can't breathe; it plugs your ears so you can no longer hear the real world and you begin to speak and think like a criminal. You look upwards and beyond that dirty pool you can only just see the faint light of the sky, and then that begins to fade fast as you sink lower and lower. That light, that glint of sky, is your old life, your real life, and you have to keep sight of that, or you might never come back..."

"It's a good analogy..." Noel begins speaking but I raise my hand to let him know I haven't finished, and he falls silent.

"99% of undercover officers know to keep the light of the sky in sight when they're immersed in the dark pool.

They make sure it's always there, that they can always see it. They complete the job and they re-surface. They wash away the filth and shit and return to their families. 99% manage to do that, but what about the other 1%?"

Noel Kelly shakes his head.

"Lenny used to say that you only come across the 1% maybe once or twice in your career. That 1% aren't just good undercover officers, they're fucking brilliant. The best. The elite. You know why Noel?"

He raises his eyebrows.

"Because that 1% aren't scared to lose sight of the sky. To sink so deep into that pool of shit that there's no light left at all, only total darkness. They're not scared of it, in fact they welcome it. It's where they feel at home. To go so deep that they can't even breathe anymore. Their eyes, mouth, ears, every part of them is so immersed in those layers of filth that it becomes them. It makes them blind, deaf, dumb. Makes them forget their old world. They've killed their old persona, their legend has become everything to them, to the point that there's nothing else left."

Any semblance of a smile has left Noel's face and he looks at me with those sad blue eyes and I can hear my grandad's voice in his soft tone.

"And that was you...You were one of the 1%."

"I still am." I look beyond the grey haired Irishman in front of me to the thin shaft of light escaping the drawn curtains.

"Once you've sunk that deep, there's no coming back."

Chapter 21

23 April 1975. The last time Leeds played in a European Cup semi-final. I was ten. My grandad got a couple of tickets off a bloke at work. I remember Andy being pissed off when my gran said he couldn't go as it was a school night. I'd been a few times before, Saturday games, but this was different. We went in the Lowfields and I can still remember climbing the steps, smelling old beer and cig smoke, reaching the terrace and looking up into the Beeston sky at those two glowing diamonds above the West Stand, casting daytime light over the emerald green pitch, the tallest fucking floodlights in the world, towering above the stadium of the soon-to-be Champions of Europe. My grandad pushing us to the front, still over an hour to kick off but the Kop already filling up. Barcelona on the pitch warming up, my grandad pointing them out, the world's greatest players, Neeskens, Asensi and the best of them all, Cruyff. I remember watching him in the warm-up, looking disinterested, probably wanting a cig, cool as fuck with his bowl cut and his shirt cuffs pulled down over his knuckles. I couldn't believe he was really there, fifty feet away from me, on a Spring night in Leeds 11. A great team, but we had nothing to fear as far as I was concerned. I was too young to realise the great Leeds team had peaked a year earlier, that maybe this final, this crowning glory of the achievements of the past decade had maybe come just too late for us.

I can't remember much of the game itself. Billy's first half top corner rocket in front of the new South Stand, and Sniffer's second half winner away to our right, lost to the memory of the subsequent celebration, the smell of oil on my grandad's donkey jacket as he wrapped his arms around me and danced with delight.

I smile at the memory as I watch a dad and son in club logo anoraks eating McDonalds on Boar Lane. Another semi-final. Another Spanish team. Another tough challenge, but at least this time no one can say the Leeds team are past their best. David O'Leary's young team, his babies, as he insists on calling them, are enjoying their big adventure in Europe, while chasing a top three league position that should secure them a place at the top table again next season.

Eddie Young yawns and taps the steering wheel of the unmarked car parked on the corner of Mill Hill.

"Fancy a walk?"

"Not bothered to be honest." I watch a couple of faces talking on phones outside the Prince of Wales. A massive game but from a disorder viewpoint it's a non-event. Valencia are only bringing a few hundred members and their FIO equivalent had laughed when I asked for details on their risk lads. It seems the Spanish haven't yet followed their Italian counterparts in developing an interest in the 'English disease.' Last time I saw the three Spanish officers sent over to cover the game, they were eating fish and chips beside the Billy Bremner statue.

I glance at my watch. 6 o'clock.

"I'd better check what the Spanish are up to. Drop me at the ground and I'll take them for a walk around, maybe pop into the Peacock with them. You come back in town and have a scan round the pubs, see who's about."

Young crunches the car into gear and we head down Mill Hill and left under the arches. I reach into my pocket for my phone and notice '1 new message received' as the screen lights up. Shivers, responding to my text asking where they are.

'Box again. meet you outside East Stand. Got sumthing 4 u.'

I begin to reply as we're passing the Hilton, but Eddie Young glances across so I slide the phone back into my jacket pocket.

I jump out of the car outside the Peacock as Eddie pulls a U-turn, and immediately spot the Spanish police and Tony Hudson chatting with the bouncers in the pub doorway. I pause next to a burger van until the unmarked car passes through the lights, then I jog across the road, glancing over my shoulder to ensure Hudson hasn't spotted me.

I pull out the Nokia next to Bremner and tap in 'here now' and push send, then fail to melt into the early pre-match crowds and one of the mounted lads from Wakey spots me and waves. I flash a thumbs up then lean into my radio and pretend to speak.

I feel the phone vibrate in my jacket and make my way towards the East Stand doors. Shivers is already pushing his way through the crowd as I arrive, the uniformed commissionaire regarding his lime green Adidas T-Master trainers and CP Company goggle-hood jacket with distaste. He's grinning as he stumbles up the steps and it's clear his pre-match refreshment session began a few hours ago.

I anticipate what's coming and grab hold of his arm as it reaches inside his jacket, steering him away from the door.

"Fuck's sake Shivers, what are you doing?"

He's laughing as I shove him into the corner near the door, the commissionaire still showing too much interest.

"I've got a present for you Charlie. Summat from Danny to tide you over."

He pulls out a folded padded envelope and leans in too close to shove it into my hand. I immediately thrust it deep into my jacket, looking over my shoulder and catching the eye of the commissionaire.

"Five hundred quid in there mate." Shivers has hold of my arm and his lips touch my ear and I can smell beer and tobacco on his breath. "Keep you going till next week. Danny's well happy with 'info you've given us."

I take a step back as he sways in front of me and run a mental calculation of how many names were on the shopping lists compared with three car boot bodies and another five shootings over the last ten days.

"Next week?" I'm shaking my head which makes him laugh even more.

"The away leg. Valencia." Shivers stumbles as he sways then steadies himself by grabbing a railing.

"I've no idea what you're on about mate." A group of suits pass us on their way down the steps and I shift my stance so it hopefully looks like I'm about to nick him for D&D.

He giggles like a schoolkid who knows a secret and slowly raises a finger to his lips and whispers an exaggerated 'Sssshhhhhh', then winks.

"Saturday. Arsenal. Danny wants to see you after 'game. He's stopping over. I'll let you know where."

I'm about to speak but he's already turning and heading back towards the East Stand doors and the commissionaire in the uniform, who's still staring at us as he reluctantly opens the door. Shivers pauses and turns towards me, pumping his right fist on his chest.

"Come on Leeds, let's have these Spanish fuckers! We are the champions, champions of Europe!"

Chapter 22

"We needed a goal, something to defend over there. I think we're fucked now." Eddie Young is perched on the edge of my desk as I stare at the computer monitor on my desk. Most of the latest comments on the Service Crew board seem to agree with him that Valencia away with the tie evenly poised at 0-0 is going to be tough.

"I've no idea how their keeper kept Matteo's header out. Then fucking Viduka slipped when Bowyer's header came off the bar. Fat Bastard."

I start laughing.

"Would you prefer him or that Carew? He was shite. Glad we never signed him."

The door opens and Carol, one of the civilian staff, pokes her orange face round the door frame and waits until the conversation subsides. It's rarely good news when someone from the office comes to see us, and everyone pauses to see who is being summoned upstairs. No surprises when her heavily mascaraed eyes turn in my direction.

"PC Mills, your presence is required in Chief Inspector Hudson's office."

Normally an invitation to Hudson's office would result in a barrage of banter and joking speculation, but everyone knows I'm well beyond that. Ginger Helen screws up her face and ducks her head behind a big white computer monitor and Eddie Young hauls himself from my desk.

"Rather you than me mate."

I climb the stairs with my stomach doing backflips and feel the perspiration soaking my palms as I make my way along the corridor. I think back to the previous night and the face of that East Stand commissionaire, the suspicion in his eyes as he watched a uniformed police officer chewing the fat with a drunken member of a criminal gang. Through the glass in the office door, I can see Hudson, flashing his tiny yellow teeth across the desk at a man in a suit facing away from me. Fuck, PSD or IOPC, it has to be.

I knock and enter and the man in the suit turns to face me. I recognise him. Millgarth CID, maybe SCS. He glances at me and nods and Tony Hudson motions for me to take the seat next to him.

"PC Mills, this is DCI Carl Daintith, Homicide and Major Crime Command." Carl Daintith extends his hand and I swivel in the seat and take it, feeling my soaked palm squelch under the pressure of his firm handshake.

"DCI Daintith is heading up the enquiry into the recent spate of shootings in the city..."

"Operation Washington." Daintith interjects.

"Ah okay, Operation Washington, DCI Daintith is heading up..." Tony Hudson carries on but Carl Daintith talks over him, turning towards me, plainly irritated that his clever op name has gone straight over Hudson's head.

"Washington...Get it?"

I do, and nod and smile politely, Hudson doesn't and looks confused, so I try to help.

"DC..."

Hudson's childlike teeth tickle his lip as his eyes flit between me and Daintith, who sighs loudly.

"DC...Danny Cade?"

Hudson's face lights up as the penny finally drops.

"Ah...Washington..DC! Cade...ha, bravo yes, very good."

"Fuck's sake." Daintith hisses under his breath, and I struggle to suppress a smirk.

"So, PC Mills, you're probably wondering why we've asked you to join us this morning, or rather, why DCI Daintith has asked to have a chat?"

I shrug, trying to appear unconcerned, although my mind is now racing with a number of possibilities, none of which are good.

Carl Daintith is clearly a man who likes to get straight to the point, and he swivels in his seat, causing the fake leather to squeak, and comes straight out with it, dropping it right on my toes.

"You know him." His eyes boring into mine cause me to look away as my heart rate surges.

"Erm, sorry, know who?" I look to Tony Hudson for a way out and he shifts in his seat, looking uncomfortable as Daintith continues.

"It's come to our attention that you have a connection with Cade going back years."

Eddie Young's obviously been chatting to his pals at Millgarth.

"Not a connection really, he went to my school, a couple of years below me."

"You knew the same people though, moved in the same circles..."

Daintith is talking to Tony Hudson rather than me, obviously hoping for some support. Hudson looks uneasy.

"Twenty years ago, maybe..."

"You're also a trained undercover operative."

"I was." I'm now looking at Hudson. He knows the back story, the PTSD, the reason I'm back up North. The child's teeth tease his bottom lip as he wriggles in his seat, his eyes flitting from Daintith to me and back again.

"I'm not sure what you're asking me..."

Daintith stands up and walks across to the window and sighs loudly as Hudson and I exchange glances. Then he turns back to face us, his hands resting on the window ledge.

"It's the usual fucking story. We're hearing whispers that Cade made some big connections while he was inside. Some serious players, and that's come to the attention of the NCIS and Europol. But for some reason, they're all keeping their cards close to their chests. They'll tell us fuck all, even though we've got dead bodies and scrotes full of bullet holes turning up all over town. We need a way in, some insight into what Cade is up to, and where Ryan Green's holed up. I'd like you on secondment, even part-time, just to have a sniff around, see what you can find..."

Tony Hudson's hands are raised before Daintith has finished talking, head shaking, toddler teeth bared, clearly not on board with Millgarth's clever plan.

"Can I stop you there Carl, couple of immediate issues with this. First, PC Mills is the FIO for Leeds United, at a time, I'm sure I don't need to point out, where the club has a huge profile in Britain and across Europe. We have a Champions League semi-final in Spain next week for God's sake."

"Obviously I'm well aware..."

Now it's Tony Hudson's turn to talk over him.

"Plus...PC Mills' transfer to WYP was a result of a conversation between DAC Rigby at the Met and ACC Brownlow. He is still receiving counselling to help overcome issues he's experienced as a direct result of his previous role with SCD10. Neither you nor I have the authority to push him back into undercover work."

Carl Daintith looks at the ceiling, then puts his hands to his head and rubs his temples while exhaling loudly. I decide to deliver the coup de grace to his plan.

"There's another problem, an even bigger one."

They both look at me expectantly.

"Some of my lads, our risk lads, are Cade's boys. There's a crossover. They know me, know I'm a copper."

Tony Hudson tries unsuccessfully to stifle a satisfied smirk as he turns to face Carl Daintith who's still leaning on the window sill.

"Sorry Carl, you know at Holbeck we'll always pitch in if we can do anything to help you. Unfortunately, this doesn't seem to be the case this time. Looks like this is one you MIT lads are going to have to solve on your own."

Chapter 23

"So...how's things?" It's the way Noel Kelly starts all our sessions.

I respond as I always do, with an ambiguous shrug.

"Same old."

He nods and smiles.

"Busy at work?"

"Yeah, I've got London on Saturday, Valencia next week. Better than sitting behind a desk though I suppose."

"Shame they couldn't have got a goal in the home leg. It's going to be tough now I think?"

I smile. "What do you know? You're an egg-chaser."

"I like to keep tabs on David and the Irish boys, my nephew Gary..."

"Is he your...?" The twinkle in Noel's eye and the barely suppressed smile tell me I've fallen for it before I've finished the sentence, and I shake my head.

"Work going okay though is it?"

I stand up and walk to the table by the window and pour myself my usual glass of water.

"They wanted me to go back undercover."

Noel doesn't respond and watches me as I walk back to the chair and sit down.

"Go on..."

"That's it. They asked me to go undercover on the op working on these shootings."

"How did you feel about that?"

"It was a non-starter. Cross-over between my current role and the targets. Some of them know I'm a copper."

Noel Kelly nods and scribbles in his pad.

"But if that hadn't been the case...?" He looks up from his notes and the question hangs between us as I consider my response.

"How would you feel if they asked you again? A different case, one where you aren't already compromised. Do you think you could ever go back?"

I bite my lip then take a sip of water.

"Do you remember what I told you last time, about the 1%?"

Noel nods slowly.

"As I said, once you've sunk so low in that dark pool that you've lost sight of the sky, there's no way back."

Noel sighs and folds his pad closed then places it on the table and turns to face me, his hands resting in his lap, pale blue eyes fixed on mine.

"I'm going to tell you what I think Charlie. You might not like it, but I'd like you to think about it carefully. It might help you decide whether going back to covert policing is really what you want to do."

"At last, the point where you tell me how mental I am and why." I smile, he doesn't.

"You've previously been diagnosed as suffering from PTSD, and I certainly think that past trauma comes into play, but in my opinion it goes beyond what happened to your partner. The death of your parents and the childhood collusion between yourself and your brother around the circumstances of the accident created a bond of guilt, a terrible secret between the two of you, a pact that reminded you both of what had occurred every time you saw each other. It was no surprise that as you both approached adulthood, you subconsciously felt the need to establish a distance between you. Tragically, that resulted indirectly in your brother losing his way and eventually taking his own life."

Noel Kelly pauses and tilts his head slightly, trying to gauge my reaction.

"Go on..." It's one of Noel's favourite phrases and it feels good to turn it back on him.

"So...there's a lot going on there. Trauma, guilt, loyalty, regret. A lot to handle for a young man, and if you bottle that up, if you don't have the right support, then those feelings can change your perception of the world, and most importantly, of yourself."

I can see he's in his element, trotting out his pseudo-psychological theory, and I don't want to piss all over his chips, I actually like the bloke, but I'd like him to get to the point.

"So, what's that all mean?"

Noel takes the point and slowly raises his hand to scratch at his grey beard.

"Okay, so here's the point Charlie. I think you've formed an opinion of yourself, maybe subconsciously. And that opinion is that you're a bad person. You dislike yourself because of what happened with your parents and your brother. The covert operations role allows you to be someone else. I'm guessing that all those officers your old boss called the 1%, they're probably all the same. For those people, it's not just a job, it's a chance to be a different person. That's why, for you, losing sight of the metaphorical sky isn't a risk of the job. It's what you want. It's why you do it."

Noel Kelly is no longer speaking in his usual soft, measured tone. He almost blurts out the last sentence, then takes a deep breath and sits back in his seat, his eyes probing mine, looking for a clue as to how I'm going to react.

I shift in my seat and gently turn the glass in my hand, watching the water as it forms a vortex. I feel like I should be angry, that I should instinctively push back against the suggestion that I'm hiding, trying to be someone else because I hate who I am, but deep down I know he's right. I only feel anything approaching happiness when I'm deep in my legend, living the life of a stranger.

I raise the glass to my lips then lower it without taking a drink.

"So, what do you expect me to do?"

Noel shakes his head and the half smile returns along with my grandfather's eyes.

"I don't expect you to do anything Charlie. Only you can decide...do you want to stay in the depths of that dark pool? Or do you want to get back to the surface and see the sky again?"

Chapter 24

"Come on then, it's a tough job but someone's got to do it." Eddie Young grins as he removes his cap and we push past the black bouncer on the door of the Flying Scotsman on Pentonville Road.

Half a dozen lads are leaning across the bar trying to catch the attention of a dead-eyed, middle aged woman who's slowly slopping flat beer into stained pint glasses. Another twenty or thirty stand in small groups in a room to the left, facing a small stage where a skinny lass with a spotty arse is gyrating half heartedly to 'Simply the Best'.

"Ey up, 'Chippendales are here." Fat Mark from Doncaster shouts from the corner of the room as we enter, and the stripper catches my eye and sticks out her tongue as she teases a nipple with a leather-gloved hand.

Mark is connected, his profile on the ITK message board makes it clear he's on good terms with lads from all over the country and beyond. He got sent down after Huddersfield in '84, and since then has become more of a hooliganism pundit than an active participant, and is always a good source of info.

"What's happening then?" I stand alongside him while Eddie walks to the front of the room and immediately gets accosted by the stripper holding out a pint glass half filled with pound coins.

"Fuck all mate, Arsenal, waste of time. Most of our lot haven't bothered today with Spain in 'week."

"You going to the game?"

Mark reaches into his pocket for a coin and drops it in the stripper's glass as she threads her way through the sparse crowd.

"I've got a ticket, I'll probably go up for a mooch about."

"Anyone else around today?" I've already checked the fixtures but Mark often comes up with something unlikely and he doesn't disappoint.

"Spurs at Leicester. They've had a bus turned back as it had a few lads on bans on it. They're heading back south now but they'll probably stop somewhere on the way. If not, they've said they might turn up down here."

I nod as if it's old news. Never show too much interest and there's a chance he'll keep talking.

"Your lot are up near 'ground." Fat Mark smirks as he turns towards the stage where a skinny, mixed-race teenager is stooping to change the tape in the ancient ghetto blaster which serves as a sound system.

"My lot?" Who's my lot?" I try to sound unconcerned. The last thing I need is him to know he's touched a nerve.

"Shivers and them. They're up on Holloway Road."

I'm about to ask what he means by 'my lot' as Eddie Young threads his way through the crowd and I feel my phone vibrating in my jacket pocket.

"Stay safe Mark." I take out the phone and nod towards the door and Eddie follows me out.

The name on the screen is Steve Milligan, and Arsenal's FIO sounds out of breath when I answer.

"Alright mate, you better get up here. It's kicked off a bit."

"Where are you?" I point down the road and we begin walking towards Kings Cross.

"George Pub, Eden Grove, just off Holloway Road. About twenty of yours and some of our youth lads. There's a van on York Way, I told them to wait for you."

"Come on, let's get a shift on." I break into a jog and Eddie and I huff and puff our way along Pentonville Road, until we see a sergeant in full robo-cop gear pacing next to a blue van.

"West Yorkshire?" He shouts across the road as we shuffle past the porn mag shop. "Come on, we'll miss all the fun."

I try texting Shivers as we cross the canal bridge on the wrong side of the road, but the blare of the siren and erratic movement of the van, plus the fact that I'm hemmed in between two lads in body armour makes it impossible. I look across at Eddie Young and he winks and smiles, eager for some action, as the radio in the front of the van crackles into life and we swerve right through an estate of three storey maisonettes. I lurch forward then back again and smash my head on the van side as we bounce over some speed bumps alongside a park. The red faced sergeant in the front seat leans back and shouts 'Arsenal are heading to the Horatia'. The lad next to me pulls on a pair of leather gloves and I'm transported back to 83, a cup game at Highbury, one of the last before I jacked it in, when 100 of us walked through these same Islington streets and bumped into Arsenal on St.Thomas's Road.

The Horatia is a grand Victorian pub on Holloway Road next to a Shell petrol station, and two mounted officers are holding a group of forty or fifty in the adjoining street when we arrive.

"This is our lot, yours are up the road." Steve Milligan emerges from the pub and points down past the garage.

"Where?" I look along the road but can't see any pubs.

"It's in a sidestreet. Couple of hundred yards, through the lights. Left where that high rise block is...fuck knows how they found it and why they're there."

I can have a pretty good guess.

"What's the betting it's just over a mile from the ground?"

"Out of the exclusion area for the banned lot."

Eddie is thinking the same as me, and we're proved right when we arrive at the pub, which is on a corner and surrounded by an uneasy mix of council maisonettes and new build yuppie flats. We push our way through a line of robocops and enter the bar to a soundtrack of agitated barking from the canine units.

It's certainly a case of quality over quantity as there are easily more officers than Leeds lads, and Shivers winks from the bar as I enter and scan the room. I count four lads who are definitely on bans and one I thought was inside. They're all top table though, and the mood is one of jovial amusement.

I give Shivers a wide berth and approach a lad called Jughead from Armley who's leaning on the window ledge, looking out at the Met officers who are staring back at him.

"Their young lads was it?"

Jughead starts laughing.

"Well it was hardly Dainton and the Herd, let's put it that way."

"They're fucking shite are Arsenal. When you think what it was like coming down here late 70's and early 80's." Craig Steel from Selby chips in from a table in the corner.

"Who called it on?" Eddie Young has pulled his cap low over his eyes to show he means business.

"Called it on? Are you having a fucking laugh? They were walking past and saw a couple of ours outside on their phones. Came bouncing over..."

"Bit off more than they could chew." Jughead lights a cigarette and blows smoke from the corner of his mouth.

"Who's got tickets?"

"I tried but I couldn't get one." Steely, who's on a five year ban grins at me and winks.

"I've got one. Me, Carl, Steve Marshall," Jughead is looking round the pub, doing a mental headcount. "And fucking Shivers and Dean Matlock are in a box again."

I raise my eyebrows.

"With Danny Cade. Someone he knows down here has one."

He watches closely to see if I react, so I make sure I don't. It seems like a good cue, so I make my way across the bar. Shivers watches me approach in the mirrored surround behind the bar.

"PC Mills. Fancy seeing you in a backstreet boozer exactly 1.1 miles from Highbury." He smiles and gestures with his eyes and the lad next to him picks up his drink and moves away.

"I hear you're in a box again today. You'll be getting used to the Corporate highlife."

"Yeah, one of Danny's mates. Someone he met in 'nick."

I look over my shoulder. Eddie Young is talking to Sergeant Milligan in the doorway.

"Where is he then?"

"Who?"

"You know who. Danny. Didn't fancy it with you lot?"

"Has to keep his nose clean doesn't he. That little carry on earlier shows why. Can't risk getting nicked over a scrap with some fucking kids can he. Not now..."

"He's down though is he?"

"Yeah, with his bird. She's shopping or something this afternoon, then they're going out with this London kid tonight."

I nod and catch Eddie Young's eye and he indicates that we're leaving, then follows Milligan out of the door.

"Shame you missed it earlier. If you'd texted me, I could have let you know where we were." Shivers turns from the bar and brushes past me, then takes my hand and shakes it firmly. "Always nice to see you Charlie."

He winks and walks towards the toilets and I clench the piece of folded paper hard in my palm and head for the pub door.

Chapter 25

"Who is he then this mate from the Met? Where's he live? What rank is he? Are you going for a meal or just a beer?"

Fuck me, you can tell Eddie Young wants to be a detective. I even thought he was going to ask if he could tag along. I'd managed to get him to cover the train home easily enough though by repeatedly asking if he thought he could handle it on his own with just BTP support.

"Course I fucking can," was the predictably over confident response.

So now I'm on my own. A quick change and scrub-up in the toilets at Kings Cross, drop my bag at left luggage and get on the Northern Line heading south. The address scribbled on the scrap of paper was Borough Market. Of course it was. New money, new ideas, new opportunity. A statement from Danny Cade. The place was a shit-hole when I first joined the Met but over the last couple of years it's been re-inventing itself as an aspirational venue for South London's bohemian foodies. Start-up businesses moving into the railway arches, throwing up a glass front, stripping the walls back to the brick and charging twenty quid for a bottle of wine or a fiver for a cocktail.

Places to see and be seen, like Black and Blue, the new 'Steak Restaurant and Cocktail bar' which I'm now standing outside, looking at my reflection in the mirrored frontage filling the arch. I know he's in there, watching me, so I take my time, inhaling my Marlboro Light slowly, watching early Saturday night drinkers picking their way down the cobbled street.

I'm tempted to light another, just to piss him off, but the door opens to allow a chattering couple to leave, so I step forward and nod at the black-clad greeter as I enter the bar and look up at the vaulted barrel ceiling.

"Can I take your jacket sir?"

I start to unzip it but then think better of it, in case I need to make a quick exit.

"No you're okay, thanks." I look at the bar, where another man in black is shaking a cocktail. Muted R&B is pitched to complement the hubbub of conversation rather than compete with it. No fucking Three Legs Elvis in here.

From the corner of my eye I notice a movement to my left and turn to see a man in a cream coloured hoodie, sunglasses on top of his head, standing, slowly extending and retracting his clenched right fist at chest level in a Leeds salute.

I climb five steps to a raised area where Cade steps forward to greet me, hand extended, his Gucci hoodie matched by a pair of cream jogging pants and large white Nikes. I resist the urge to smirk, remembering him wearing similar gear in the Chained Bull fifteen years ago. Still no fucking idea.

"Charlie..." He smiles a too-white smile, looks hard into my eyes as he grips my right hand with his, and places his left hand on my shoulder.

"What you drinking mate?" He raises a finger and a black clad Chinese girl hurries up the steps towards us.

"A bottle of lager's fine for me thanks."

"Bottle of lager, a coke and...same for you Jay?" He turns towards a table behind us and a thin, bespectacled black man in his late twenties raises a glass.

"And a rum and coke please love."

The Chinese girl scurries away and Danny Cade guides me towards the table where the black man remains seated.

"Charlie, this is Jay. Jay, Charlie Mills."

I extend my hand and the black man slowly lifts a fist and holds it six inches from my fingertips, so I clench my fingers and awkwardly tap my knuckles on his.

Danny Cade smiles and pulls out a chair and I sit down.

"Fucked that up today, didn't we? Load of shite." Cade is one of those people who pretends to be into football but doesn't really understand it, and I surprise myself by launching into a defence of Leeds' performance.

"Keown should have been sent off for that elbow on Viduka, then the stamp on Kewell. We missed Batty though, Bakke struggled."

"Fourth now, and our goal difference is shit compared to Liverpool isn't it? We've fucked it I reckon. Need to win in Spain next week now or it's the UEFA cup next season." Cade shakes his head, and the Chinese girl appears with three glasses on a tray. I can feel the weight of the black man's stare as I pick up a bottle of Michelob and slowly fill a half glass.

"Anything else gentlemen?" The girl smiles and Danny Cade raises a hand and shakes his head and the three of us watch her make her way back down the steps to the bar.

The black man picks up his empty glass and tips the ice into the new drink and slowly stirs it with a straw, and I look at Danny Cade and he looks at me, but no one speaks. The black man raises his glass to his lips and takes a sip then slowly places it back on the black marble table top and looks at me, while flicking his tongue over his lips.

"So, Charlie, you're the man then, is what I'm hearing." His voice is soft, south London with a slight lisp. He's dressed all in black. A smart shirt, open at the neck under a narrow lapelled jacket and a fat diamond in his ear. A gold-capped front tooth catches the light from a halogen bulb above us as he speaks.

I'm considering how to respond when Danny Cade jumps in.

"Charlie has proved his worth since I got out. We couldn't have got to the point we're at now up north without the information he's provided."

The black man nods and narrows his eyes as he looks me up and down.

"So what is it you want me to do then?"

The black man is laughing now, turning towards Cade.

"You haven't told him. Fucking hell..."

Cade sighs and slowly lifts his right hand from the chair arm, and moves it like he's patting an invisible dog in the space between them.

"Chill out Jay, we agreed we'd do this face to face."

An uneasy feeling ripples deep in my stomach and I breathe in through my nose and count to four. Hold for six. Exhale for four.

Jay is laughing quietly to himself, shaking his head as Danny Cade shifts forward in his seat.

"So...Charlie. As you know, we've been clearing the decks up north. Jay has been doing the same on his patch down here, and we're nearly there now. It's time for phase 2 of the plan to begin."

I pick up my glass quickly and hold it in both hands to stop them shaking.

"What is phase 2?"

Danny Cade looks at Jay who stares at the barman shaking the cocktails, seemingly removing himself from the discussion, and I wonder if he thinks I'm wired up.

"As I told you before, because the coke market has evolved so quickly here, it's fragmented, disorganised, chaotic. Run by different firms, with different supply routes. We spend more time competing with each other than selling. Turf battles, price wars, grassing to your lot. Petty arguments between small firms with local grudges. What we're planning is a consolidated approach. Us in the north and Jay's group in the south with a single source of supply, the best product that's ever been sold in Britain. Once we're set up, all the rest will fall into line, the scousers and mancs, the jocks, the geordies..."

"Makes sense..." I take a swig of my beer, trying not to appear too interested, too desperate.

"I told you I made connections when I was inside, Jay here is one. We were in Long Lartin together. There was a lad called Custer from the Caribbean, Belize. He was awaiting extradition to Spain and the three of us got our heads together. He was connected..." Danny Cade pauses and looks at Jay, who slowly turns back towards us and takes a slow sip of his rum and coke before speaking quietly.

"VERY connected."

Danny nods and carries on.

"I'll cut a long story short...Custer knew someone who was looking for a way into the UK market, if they could find the right partners. Custer vouched for us and Jay started working with them on the detail when he got out a few months ago. It's all in place now."

"So what do you need me for?" I can feel my heart beating hard in my chest and the glass is sticking to the sweat on my palms.

Danny exchanges glances with Jay, and the black man shuffles forward towards me so I can smell the old weed on his clothes. He extends his right hand and places it on my arm.

"We need to move some cash. A lot of cash."

"Move it where?"

Jay sits back and Danny Cade takes over again.

"As you can imagine Charlie, there are significant set up costs with an major operation like this. Storage facilities, boats, crews, officials to be bought off in different countries. Our partners need to see the funding upfront, and this isn't the sort of money you keep in your Yorkshire Bank savings account, so you can't just write a cheque or do a bank transfer. This is a cash transaction and the cash needs to be with our partners in Spain."

"How much?"

Danny Cade looks at Jay who narrows his eyes and looks back towards the bar.

"You don't need to know that."

"So, what's my involvement?"

Danny Cade leans forward again.

"The semi-final next week."

"What about it?" I can see where this is going and I don't like it.

"When are you flying out?"

"Monday morning. Charter flight for the club officials, local press and coppers."

Danny Cade nods and smiles and exchanges a 'told-you-so' glance with Jay.

"You'll be carrying a special bag that we'll provide. It's top gear, with a sealed false bottom. A fucking money dog could have its nose right in there and all he'll be sniffing is your soiled boxers."

It's my turn to laugh now.

"Are you fucking joking?"

Danny isn't smiling anymore.

"No joke Charlie. It's foolproof. Customs aren't going to stop a copper and if they do, this bag is top notch. They...our partners are providing it."

"And who are they? You never said."

"You don't need to..." Danny is shaking his head.

"CDS. Cartel de Sinaloa. Pacific Cartel." Jay lisps the letters quietly and I turn towards him. "

"Mexicans then, not Columbians?"

"Mexicans are going to be the new power. Columbia has imploded since Escobar died." Jay sips at his drink and looks hard into my eyes, trying to gauge my reaction.

"Ten grand. Cash." Danny Cade clasps his hands together as if in prayer and rests his chin on them.

"What? In the bag?" As soon as I've said it, they're both pissing themselves laughing.

"Fuck me Charlie, I wish it was only ten grand in the bag, but that wouldn't go far on setting something like this up. That's your fee mate." Cade looks at me like a proud father watching his kid find a bike under the tree on Christmas morning.

"Ten grand? To take the bag to Valencia?" I feel more of a twat because I've walked right into it, and they can tell from my reaction I wasn't expecting anything like that amount.

Danny Cade nods.

"You take the bag through customs and deliver it to my man over there on Monday night. You'll get ten grand cash when you're back in Leeds and the money is with the Mexicans."

"We're not in Valencia on Monday. We fly into Alicante and I'm staying in Benidorm, that's where our main lads are going."

Danny Cade is laughing again.

"Do you think I'm not ITK Charlie? I know everyone's going to Benidorm. You'll be meeting my uncle Terry at his hotel there. Do you remember him?" He hands over a scrap of paper with *'Hotel Victoria. Avenida Emilio Ortuno'* written on it.

"No I don't think so."

"He's lived over there for ten years now, but he was one of the main lads in town in the early eighties. Surprised you don't remember him."

I shake my head and try not to think about some clever bastard customs officer at LBA working out that my bag is a bit too heavy for a change of clothes and a bag of toothpaste and deodorant.

"Where's this bag then?"

"Shivers has it. He'll meet you on Monday morning early."

"Monday morning? We fly out at ten."

"As I said, early. We can't risk leaving this sort of money in your gaff overnight. The less time you have it, the better for everyone. Understand?"

I'm about to say I do, when I feel the weight of Jay's hand on my arm. His grip tightens as he leans towards me, and my nostrils are filled with the stink of old weed again. His voice is still soft and lisping, almost a whisper.

"Danny tells me he trusts you, Charlie." His eyes narrow behind the thick rim of his glasses and his hand closes tighter on my forearm. "And I trust Danny. I don't know you though."

The background R&B is the only sound for a few seconds as I shift uneasily under the weight of Jay's hand on my arm, then the Nokia ring tone beeps out from the pocket of Cade's hoodie and he stands and places a finger to his left ear. Jay leans in even closer so I can feel his breath on my cheek.

"You've got my money there Charlie, all my fucking money. Please don't let us down, or things are going to go very badly for you very quickly. Alright?"

I nod and catch Danny's eye as he looks from Jay to me and back again, the phone held to the side of his head, a smile spreading across his face.

He steps back towards the table and Jay releases his grip from my arm, but I can feel the weight of his stare from behind the lens of his glasses. Danny Cade holds the Nokia out towards me, and I see two letters on the illuminated green screen.

'RG'

RG. Ryan Green. The man marking my homework. Danny Cade has the phone to his ear, grinning, laughing now like he wants everyone to ask him what the joke is.

"Did he?...fucking hell...the wanker...what did he do then?...Ha, ha, ha..."

Danny Cade tosses his head back and laughs too loud, causing the Chinese waitress to turn and look in our direction. Jay picks up his Rum and Coke and takes a sip but doesn't shift his eyes from my face.

"Fucking top job mate...yeah, great work....in London...with our lass...I'm with Jay now actually...bar near London Bridge...no, just me him and Charlie...the copper, you know..."

Danny Cade's smile slips and he winks at me.

"Yeah hang on...I'll put him on." Danny Cade puts his hand over the phone. "It's Ryan, he wants a word."

"What with me?" I feel my stomach lurch and my chest tighten. I don't have time to breathe as he hands me the phone.

"Is that the copper?" Ryan Green's voice crackles down the line and I have to put a finger in my left ear to hear him.

"Yeah, it's Charlie, you alright?"

"I'm alright charver, do you know where I am?"

"Erm no..."

"I'm outside 'Crown, over 'road from Clyde Court at Wortley. Do you know Clyde Court?"

I know Clyde Court, just off Tong Road. A high rise Leeds City Council dumping ground for druggies, burglars, single mothers and unfortunate pensioners, and I also know why he's asking.

"Yeah, I know it. It was on the list."

"Well done Charlie, you remembered. Can you remember who lived there?"

Lived there. Not lives. I feel the nausea rising in my throat and inhale deeply for a count of four. Hold for two, exhale quickly and silently as Danny Cade and Jay are staring right at me.

"Craig Marshall."

"Correct again! You're good at this Charlie. Little Craig had his first flying lesson about half an hour ago, and his last. Maybe he shouldn't have tried off the eleventh floor to begin with, eh?" Ryan Green laughs until he coughs himself to a stop.

"Anyway Charlie, we're getting to the end of your lists now, and I understand you've got a promotion, which is a good thing."

He seems to be waiting for a response, but I don't know what to say other than okay.

"Do you want to know why it's a good thing Charlie?"

Danny Cade motions for me to hand him the phone back, but I can't help myself saying that yes, I do want to know.

"Because if there's one thing I hate more than coppers it's fucking bent coppers, and if Danny wasn't relying on you for next week, I'd put a bullet in both your knees and another one in your ball-sack... See you soon Charlie."

I hand the phone back to Danny Cade and try to reach out for my beer bottle, but my hand is shaking too much to raise it above the table. Danny laughs and smiles and says his goodbyes then puts the phone back in his hoodie and sits down.

"Okay Charlie. That's another job done. Another obstacle out of the way. As you probably know, my parole conditions prevent me from leaving the country, so I can't go to the game. Next time we meet it will be when you get back from Spain, and I'll give you your cash."

He stands up and extends his hand, telling me it's time to go. I stand up, shake Cade's hand and turn towards Jay. He takes a sip of his drink and looks at his shoes as Danny places a hand on my shoulder.

"Good luck Charlie. Let's hope we get the right result in Spain."

As I head towards the steps I hear a soft south London voice behind me.

"Because if we don't, it's fucking over for all of us."

Chapter 26

"But I don't understand how this Manchester company could advertise a package with match tickets before we even knew how many Leeds were getting. It's bloody ludicrous."

It's 7.30 in the morning and we're standing outside the main doors of the terminal at Leeds Bradford airport. Tony Hudson's tiny yellow teeth are dancing between his lips amidst a canopy of stringy saliva which is making my nausea even worse. My head is thumping from the eight pints of Stella and two litres of Frosty Jack I drank to try and get some sleep before my 5am meeting with Shivers.

"Fat Malcolm, he's a ticket tout, he has contacts all over Europe." Talking makes my throat sore and I'm gagging for a smoke but Hudson has already made it clear we're on duty even though we aren't in uniform.

"And how many do we think are on this two night package of his?"

I know exactly how many are on the Connected Travel trip with one night in a 4-star hotel at Benidorm's Levante beach tonight, followed by a night in Valencia city centre tomorrow. Lee Molloy is a good mate of Fat Malcolm's and has sent me the full list of names who've signed up at £379 plus £40 for a match ticket in the Valencia end, and are flying out from Manchester in a couple of hours.

"About fifty I think."

"And there are Cat C's among them?"

"A handful sir, yes." I don't mention that I've already met four of them this morning, when they stopped on their way to the M62 to hand over a brown leather holdall containing a six figure sum of drug money for a Mexican cartel.

"Ludicrous. I need you to be all over this group tonight and tomorrow...ah, about time, they're here now."

Hudson nods towards a black and white Telecabs taxi from which Eddie Young and EGT Pierre are clambering. The young Frenchman is lugging a heavy metal box of photographic equipment.

"About time, PC Young, the club staff checked in twenty minutes ago and I've just seen that Rostron and his photographer checking in."

We make our way through the sliding doors, past the deserted W.H.Smiths and Boots shops to the check-in area, where three gypsies in cheap suits and a pension-aged couple are loitering, waiting for the Aer-Lingus check-in to open. I glance at the departure board. A Thompson flight to Heraklion departed half an hour ago; Dublin at 10.30; British Midland to Paris at 11.15; AirTours to Tenerife at 13.15. A busy morning at Yorkshire's premier airport, with our 'Special Charter' undoubtably a highlight for the under employed staff.

A smiling late thirties woman in a cheap nylon uniform greets us and asks us if we have any bags to check in. Hudson has made clear that we're travelling hand luggage only, and he huffs and tuts when the woman tells us that Pierre's metal camera box will need to go in the hold.

"Ridiculous. That's police equipment. I hope for your sake it doesn't suffer any damage." The woman catches my eye and raises an eyebrow, but I can't even manage a half smile as I'm focusing on retaining control of my bowels. My stomach is churning like a washing machine and the nausea is rising in my chest at the prospect of the Mexicans' 'special bag' making its way through the customs x-ray machine.

I've decided to avoid being the first or last to pass through security, so position myself behind Tony Hudson and Eddie Young and in front of Pierre as we file along towards the scanner, where two overweight men in uniform, one of whom turns out to be a woman, are scowling and monitoring our approach.

"Alicante is it gents?" The officer with the heavier moustache of the two takes a grey tray from a conveyor belt and hands it to Tony Hudson, who thankfully wastes no time in letting them know exactly who we are.

"West Yorkshire Police football liaison unit. I'm Chief Inspector Hudson based at Holbeck and these are my support team."

Fucking support team. Hudson has managed to persuade his opposite number in Valencia that he needs to attend to 'share intelligence and best practice', which will no doubt translate as two nights in the city's best seafood restaurants on expenses, while we get run ragged on the streets. I'm wondering whether they have Freemasons in Spain as Hudson and Eddie Young's bags disappear into the scanner and I place mine in a tray and shove it in after them.

I smile weakly at the ambiguously sexed customs officer and try hard to control my breathing as the holdall disappears and the machine whirrs and buzzes. I glance over at the operator, a thin young man with glasses and receding hair, and run the back of my hand across my sweating forehead. He looks focused and unusually efficient for Leeds Bradford, and I feel my stomach lurch as his eyes flit across the screen and he taps a keyboard and the scanner stops whirring. Another tap results in another mechanical noise, this time higher pitched, and I watch in horror as the conveyor belt jerks back into reverse.

Fuck, fuck, fuck...I feel like I'm going to vomit and stare hard at Eddie Young's back as he lifts his bag from the conveyor belt. Obviously British scanners are more high tech than the shite they have in Mexico, and the young man is now probably staring hard at the dozens of mysterious dark bundles showing up on his screen in the bottom of my bag. I realise I haven't even bothered to come up with a story to explain the cash when I'm caught, and I feel dizzy and close my eyes as he taps the keyboard again and the conveyor belt stops, then starts again. He's leaning forward looking at the screen, squinting through narrowed eyes, and I know the game is up. My mouth feels so dry I can barely move my tongue to lick my lips.

I'm staring ahead, but sense a movement and glance over to see the young man take a swig from a coffee mug, then look back at his screen as my bag emerges from the scanner. I exhale so loudly that Pierre glances in my direction as he waits for his bag. I smile and wink.

"Starving mate, hope we've got time for a bacon sarnie?"

Chapter 27

"This looks like our man now." Tony Hudson has his M&S anorak over his arm and has put on a pair of fake Ray-Bans to scan the approaching traffic outside Arrivals at Alicante Airport.

He raises his arm and a blue Mercedes people carrier flashes its lights and begins to slow down.

"So, PC Mills, as agreed you'll be covering Benidorm tonight in support of the Policia Nacional. Stay in touch and keep us updated and we'll do the same, then we'll rendezvous in Valencia tomorrow."

The justification for three officers basing themselves in Valencia and leaving only me in Benidorm is that Valencia police are calling the shots, and we had to argue to have anyone in Benidorm at all. In reality, Hudson wants maximum cover where he is, so he can fuck off and have a two day holiday. Suits me though and I nod my assent and watch them climb into the van, then wave them off. I walk back into Arrivals and buy two bottles of San Miguel from a snack bar. I sink one in three gulps, knock the top off the other and walk to the taxi rank.

I tuck the open bottle into my jacket pocket as I duck into the back seat, and hand over a WYP headed memo showing the name of my hotel. Hotel Caballo de Oro, Avenida Cuenca. The driver peers at the address through a pair of readers perched on the end of his nose and grunts an acknowledgement.

"Playa Levante?"

He looks at me in the rear view mirror but doesn't respond. I've made it clear to Carol in the office that I need a hotel close to the lads on Fat Malcolm's trip and near where most of the other Leeds lads will be staying tonight.

"This hotel...it's at Playa Levante?"

He replies in Spanish and looks in the mirror again. I shrug. I wasn't expecting a seaview room but forty minutes later we're pulling up in a long road of high-rise holiday flats and I haven't even caught a glimpse of the Mediterranean.

The driver points upwards and I follow his finger to gaze up at a 10 storey block with six foot blue letters saying 'Hotel' on the roof. Clearly, the budget didn't stretch to getting anywhere near the beach.

I check in and suss out the room. No safe, so I take off the bath panel and stuff the bag in there, then take out my phone and dial the number I've been given for my contact.

'Lorenzo Pérez, Sargento de la Policia Nacional.'

He doesn't answer so I leave a message and set off out to see who's about. Ten minutes later I'm furtively swigging a pint at Andy's bar, having swerved the Yorkshire Pride over the road where fifteen lads from Batley are already stacking up the empties on a line of tables.

My phone buzzes and a Spanish number flashes up, Sergeant Pérez no doubt, so I kill the call. I'm not meeting Cade's uncle till 8pm so there's plenty of time for a few pints and a mooch around to see who's here. Then a quick hook-up with the Spanish plod, make my excuses, scoot back to the hotel to retrieve the cash, then back out in plenty of time for the meeting.

More lads are arriving at the Yorkshire Pride, the old school cool of Head bags tempered by a smattering of wheely suitcases from the younger ones. I decide there's too much chance of being spotted here so I turn left up Calle Gerona, ducking my head as I pass the Dublin House and Shamrock bars, from where the first strains of 'We are Leeds' are already competing with 'Believe' by Cher, pumping from the speakers.

I follow the road to a roundabout at its end, where the outdoor seating of Captain Morgan's Tavern is positioned on the deck of a fake pirate ship, ten feet above the road. A perfect vantage point to see and not be seen, so I duck into the bar, the smell of bleach fighting a losing battle with old beer and sweat and vomit.

It's two for one until 7pm, and I've nearly finished my first pint of San Miguel by the time I pull up a chair on the fake galleon's port side, and watch the traffic negotiating the roundabout. I'm half way down the second pint when the Nokia buzzes again and the Spanish number appears on the screen.

"Hola?" It's more or less the extent of my Spanish language skills so I may as well use it.

"PC Mills? This is Lorenzo Pérez from CNP. Have you arrived?"

He speaks good English with a noticeable Spanish lisp.

"Yes, I've just arrived at the hotel, just checking in." I swill back the rest of the pint and glance at my watch.

"Shall we meet you there? What is the name?"

"Erm...yes, that's fine. The Hotel is Caballo de Oro, Avenida Cuenca. I just need to make a call to my boss first. Shall we say 16.00 in the foyer?"

By the time he's agreed and confirmed where the hotel is, I'm already halfway down the steps to the bar.

"Same?" says the eastern European girl behind the counter.

Might be the last chance I have to grab some food before tonight, and I pause and skim read the marker-pen menu on a whiteboard behind her.

"Maybe need something to line my stomach....make it two pints of Guinness love please."

Chapter 28

"So, football police work is your whole job? You don't have to do anything else?"

Lorenzo Pérez turns from the front seat of the unmarked BMW and smiles incredulously. I suck hard on an Extra-Strong Mint and nod and shrug and he starts to laugh, then jabbers away in Spanish to Alvaro in the driver's seat next to him. Alvaro laughs too as we pull away from the hotel and head along Avenida Cuenca.

"Alvaro says it sounds like the sort of job the police commissioner would give to his son. You're not related to the boss are you?"

"Quite the opposite actually. You could say I'm not exactly flavour of the month with my boss."

Alvaro speaks again and Lorenzo translates.

"Alvaro works for SATE. They only deal with foreign tourists so it's seen as an easy job. He's asking if you want to swap with him?"

"Pissed up Brits every night? No thanks, I'd rather stick with our hooligans."

Lorenzo faces forward again and turns down the radio, calling back over his shoulder.

"So your intelligence says some of your hooligans will be here tonight?"

"Yeah, I know of a couple of groups staying here who could cause problems. Valencia police are telling us they don't really have a large risk group so I'm not sure why they wanted three of our officers there tonight. I think there's likely to be more action here."

Lorenzo mutters to Alvaro and he slows the car down at a roundabout, from where I get my first glimpse of the distant Mediterranean between two tower blocks at the end of the road. Lorenzo is looking left and tapping on the window, pointing towards a corner bar called Vesta Café.

"These boys will be the problem, not Valencia supporters."

A dozen young men are loitering around two empty tables. Dark skinned, with complexions ranging from the olive skin of Morocco to the dark black of sub-Saharan Africa, they listlessly monitor the street, smoking and chatting. Some are stooping over brightly coloured bundles from which they remove sunglasses and wood carvings which they polish with stained towels.

"Are they going to be wanting to fight do you think?"

Lorenzo rolls down the window and we wait until a couple of the lads see him and scowl and nod before we pull away.

"Not so much to fight, but to rob a drunken tourist. They use the hookers as decoys. And when your supporters try to help their friend, then they'll fight. They all carry knives too."

I puff out my cheeks and exhale loudly and Lorenzo understands.

"For your team, after Turkey, not a good situation."

We turn right and park at the bottom of Avenida de Filipinas and I can already hear chants of

'Yorkshire...Yorkshire' as I clamber out of the back seat opposite the Tiki bar.

"A few of your boys are outside the Dunes Bar." Lorenzo leads the way onto the seafront promenade Avenida de Madrid, and points upwards at a dozen Union Jacks and St. George crosses flying from the balconies of the twenty-storey Dunes Suites. More flags line the patio overlooking Levante beach, where around fifty lads are drinking. I scan the flags before the faces. Newark, Great Harwood, Hunslet, Cross Gates and a Welsh dragon from Ebbw Vale. Nothing to concern me, but then I spot the grinning skull of a Seacroft Mentals flag at the far side of the patio but I can't see whose it is.

Our presence has been noted and the usual dance begins as a few of the 'Plod's Pals' lads try to catch my eye, and I notice a couple of others disappear at speed towards the toilets inside the bar. Banned lads were meant to surrender their passports before today but the system isn't foolproof, and if Eddie Young was here he'd have been straight after them. I can't be arsed, so I have a slow walk through the crowd, with Lorenzo and Alvaro following.

"Got a nice room Charlie? Sea View I bet?"

Glen Ramsden from Holt Park is a proper Plod's Pal, wears the gear but is generally no bother at all, so I give him what he wants.

"Yeah, penthouse suite Rammer, infinity pool on the balcony, personal butler and in-room masseuse, and d'you know the best thing about it?"

"Yeah, us taxpayers are paying for your holiday!"

"Exactly."

I head over to the Seacroft flag. A few old 70's and 80's lads from Leeds 9 and Beeston, out of retirement for the big game, a couple who I know from the old Precinct days but haven't seen at a match since I started the job.

"Alright Neil..."

A flicker of recognition appears on Neil Yardsley's face and he smiles.

"Fuck me, Charlie Mills. I heard a rumour you'd changed sides..."

"Times change mate. Didn't know you still came?"

"I don't. Not been for nearly ten years and I haven't got a ticket. Danno's getting married again though, so we thought we'd have the stag do here."

I assess the table. No Plod's Pals here, no smiles or in-jokes, just scowls and silence from old school lads more used to the days before football intelligence.

"You lot going to Valencia or staying here tomorrow?"

"I wasn't bothered but the younger lads want to go." Neil Yardsley shrugs. "Got to be better than here, hasn't it?"

"How many do you think will be here without tickets?" Lorenzo scans the faces at the table as he appears next to me.

"Couple of thousand maybe. They won't all be trying to go to the game though, a lot will be happier watching in a bar."

Alvaro's radio crackles and he leans in towards his breast pocket to listen to the undecipherable jabber of the operator, then mutters to Lorenzo who tilts his head to indicate that it's time to go.

"Let's take a walk up to the strip, a couple of the bars have called in to say it's getting a little...interesting up there."

I glance at my watch. Not even 5pm yet.

"I think it's going to be a long night." Lorenzo calls over his shoulder as we head towards the street.

You can say that again.

Chapter 29

Hotel Victoria. Avenida Emilio Ortuno. I lean against a phone box and look up at the illuminated multi-storey tower looming high above me. I take a last drag on my Marlboro Light, drop it on the floor along with my last three tab ends, and put it out with my shoe.

I look at my watch. 19.57. Nearly time. I inhale slowly through my nose, hold for six then exhale, and repeat. I wipe my hands on my jeans then rub them together in a vain attempt to get rid of the moisture. He's bound to want to shake hands and the thought of that makes me sweat even more.

I've been told to meet him in the restaurant, and I peer at the tinted glass frontage as I approach, looking for a clue on which way to head once I'm through the door. There's a palm shaded terrace to the right of the door with tables for four, covered by large white square parasols, and as I hesitate at the entrance I glance right and immediately catch his eye. It's been over twenty years, but I recognise him immediately and my stomach turns to liquid. Grey moustache and a faded but still-visible scar across his cheek. No big gold ear-ring anymore, still looks like Yozzer Hughes though. Uncle Terry. Terry Cade. TC. The Whip, Starlight Rooms, NF News and Bulldog on the Lowfields, Potty Park and petrol bombs. Andy with a belt round his neck at Kirklevington. I realise I've stopped walking and struggle to catch my breath. He's realised I'm the connection and he's saying something to the man with his back to me. The other man turns round, mid-fifties, purple face, shaved head. TC raises his eyebrows and tilts his head, telling me to join them and I coax my legs slowly forward, gripping the handle of the hold-all in sweat-soaked hands.

He watches, unsmiling, as I approach, his eyes flicking from mine to the bag and back, walrus moustache and sun-burnished scar marking a face cast in a permanent sneer.

"You're the copper." His lip curls in distaste beneath its greying canopy, and the other man tilts his head towards me and grunts.

"Charlie..." I hold out the bag towards him and Terry Cade nods to the other man, and he reaches out to take it, then places it under the table.

I remain standing, looking down at this ghost from my past, who I've tried to put out of my mind, but could never quite forget, and I stare down at him in horrified fascination.

Terry Cade picks up a bottle of Estrella from the table and tips the dregs into his glass, then looks at me again, seemingly irritated that I'm still there.

"You can go now."

I shift my feet but don't move.

"Don't you want to check it?"

TC smirks and picks up his glass.

"The bottom of that bag is sealed. Believe me, if anyone has tried to open it, you'll be finding out about it very quickly mate."

He takes a sip of his beer then licks the froth off his moustache. His eyes suggest he's about to tell me to fuck off and my brain is racing and before I can stop myself, I've said it.

"I remember you."

The bald man shifts in his seat and looks up at me then back at Terry Cade, who lowers his eyebrows and stares hard into my eyes.

"Oh aye. From where?"

I've said it now and there's no going back and my mind is scrambling to re-engage.

"Early 80's. The Whip, NF and that. I was one of the younger lads who used to sell the papers outside Elland Road."

The bald man sighs loudly and swigs from his beer bottle as Terry Cade narrows his eyes and tilts his head as if to get a better look at me. He shakes his head.

"Nah...don't remember."

"I was Andy's mate. We were skinheads..." I think I notice his left eye twitch when I mention the name but convince myself I've imagined it.

"Andy who?" Terry Cade reaches up and rubs at his tash.

"I can't remember his name. He went to my school. I lost track of him when I left. Wondered if you knew what happened to him."

He pauses and I watch his Adam's Apple move up and down and his nostrils flare slightly. Then he shakes his head.

"No...don't remember any Andy. There were lots of young skins around then though." He picks up his bottle again. "Anyway, hadn't you better be getting off? There'll be plenty of pissed-up lads for you and your Spanish mates to batter tonight."

I smile but he doesn't and neither does the bald man, who taps the bag with his foot until it disappears under the table.

"Okay, so you'll let Danny know, I've made the drop?"

"You'll get your money kid, don't worry. Now fuck off."

Chapter 30

I walk away from the terrace of the Victoria Hotel and pause on the corner, then put my hands on my thighs and lean forward and watch as Guinness tainted vomit splashes onto the pavement and my trainers. My heart is thumping in my chest, and I have to grip a roadside railing to steady myself as the tower blocks above me begin to spin. I glance back to the terrace and see Terry Cade and the bald man laughing at the table. Two black prostitutes are watching me from the other side of the road as I take the Marlboro packet from my jacket and light one with a shaking hand.

I balance the cig between my lips, and remove my wallet under a street lamp, then take out two fifty Euro notes and three twenties. I hold them up to the light and count them slowly, then put them back in my wallet, and carefully slide it into the front pocket of my jeans. I step off the kerb and stagger slightly, gripping the railing again to steady myself.

I hear chanting from further down the street and raise my arms and join in. *'Manchester can rave about the Summerbee and Best, then there's Liverpool and Arsenal and Spurs and all the rest...*

Out of the corner of my eye, I see the two girls approaching, one walking a couple of metres in front of her friend.

'...but let us sing the praises of the lads we love the best, as Leeds go marching on...'

The first girl is alongside me now, early twenties, hair scraped back in a tight bun and wearing denim shorts and a white vest top.

"Where are you going?" She speaks in the clipped tones of West African English and her nipples are prominent beneath her t-shirt.

"I'm off to meet my mates. Where are you going?"

She smiles the perfect white smile of a child who grew up without ever tasting Mars Bars or Coca Cola.

"We're going to a party, me and my sister." She turns and the other girl flashes a similar white smile accompanied by a coy wave. "Do you want to come and party with us?"

"I'd love to girls, but I think I've had enough to drink today." I set off walking and the first girl is alongside me, linking her right arm through mine.

"Come on, you want to party with me and my sister? We have an apartment, we can go there now."

The other girl speeds up and she is walking on my right, and she reaches over and squeezes my arse cheek and winks.

"Don't you like my sister?" the girl on the left pulls me closer and now I see them. Three black lads leaning on a wall at the other side of the road.

"You like massage? My sister gives good massage." The girl grips my arm and moves her left hand towards my crotch, brushing my balls as I try to push her away.

"You have a nice ass." The other girl has now rested her hand on my buttock and is stealthily checking my back pockets. I turn and brush her off and she backs away laughing.

"Don't you like sexy girls?" The first girl is gyrating in front of me, running her hands over her breasts then down between her legs and I feel her friend's hands making a grab for my front pocket. I'm backing away now towards the wall.

"No, fuck off...get away from me!"

"What's wrong with you? We just want to party with you." The girls are closing in like predators, smiling, swaying, eyes probing my defences for signs of weakness. My back is against the wall and I turn and begin fast walking back the way I've come, and I can hear them close behind me.

"Hey, what's wrong, don't you like sexy girls? Do you like boys? We know sexy boys..."

I slow down as I reach the corner and glance over my shoulder. The girls are still following and have now been joined by two of the lads. I bend down to tie my lace and wipe a fleck of black vomit from the instep of my trainer. Before I've stood up, I feel a knee in my back.

"What you say to my sister?"

I slowly stand and turn to face him. He's tall, mid-twenties with a Real Madrid beanie hat pulled low over his forehead.

"What? I didn't say anything..."

I look at the girls who are leaning on the wall, staring, scowling. No white teeth on show now. The other lad steps forward and prods me in the chest.

"They say you're a faggot."

"No, I'm not a faggot."

The first youth now has hold of my arm.

"You make insult to my sister. You have to pay her money."

I start laughing, and shake my head, but before I've had chance to speak, there's an explosion of pain on my temple and I see stars and reel backwards and land on the pavement. The third youth has come from nowhere and blindsided me with a punch to the side of the head. I feel hands probing my jeans pockets so I roll onto my front. They seem to pause, then one lands a kick, hard in my ribs. We're suddenly lit up in the headlights of a passing car and they take a step back, which allows me to use the wall to push myself up so I'm standing in front of them.

The first lad steps forward again and takes hold of my arm.

"You make insult, you must pay." I can smell spirit on his breath and he sprays saliva into my face as he speaks.

"Okay, okay, I'll pay. Please just don't..."

His face is so close to mine that I have to take a step back before I can head-butt him. My forehead connects with his nose, sending blood spraying over both of us. He instantly releases his grip on my arm and I try to kick him in the balls but miss. I set off running and one of the other lads manages to clip my ankle and I go down, roll, then regain my footing and set off running back towards the hotel. I think I might have cracked a rib and clutch my chest as I run, and I can taste the salty blood from the African's nose on my lips. I can hear them coming behind me and am out of breath when I reach the hotel entrance.

I stop, turn and face them.

"Fucking come on then!" I roar at the top of my voice and hurl myself forward, glancing a punch off the cheekbone of an advancing African. One of his mates launches a flying kick at my head. I dodge that but the other lad has hold of my jacket collar and is raining punches on the back of my head. I'm in trouble and wondering if I've made a mistake, when the battering suddenly ends and I look up to see the bald man with the purple face advancing with fists held at chest level.

"Come on then you black bastards, three against three now!" Terry Cade also appears alongside me brandishing a leather belt with a heavy brass buckle which he spins around his head. The lad with the broken nose still seems game and bounces forward, dodging a couple of haymakers from the bald man before picking him off with three well aimed jabs. Whether TC's belt was ever an effective weapon in a street fight is debatable, but now, in the hands of a middle-aged man, it's next to useless. In a matter of seconds it's in the hands of one of the Africans and Terry is retreating rapidly, trying to dodge the flailing buckle end. Things are going according to plan, so I back off from the lad who's ducking and bobbing in a boxing stance in front of me. He follows me onto the terrace and I pick up a chair and launch it at his head, then while he's dodging that, I hurtle forward and land a flying kick in the small of his back to send him crashing backwards, taking a table of empties with him.

I glance across to the road to where Terry Cade is cowering as a lanky black kid flails at him with the belt. I pick up an Estrella bottle and jog forward, timing my approach perfectly, to bring the bottle down on the back of the lad's head just before he sees me coming. He turns, eyes wide with shock, and sets off running in the split second before the blow registers on his brain and deprives him of his sense of co-ordination. He spins sideways, hits a parked car and lands on his back in the gutter. The Estrella bottle has smashed, leaving me holding the neck and remaining half of its jagged body, so I step forward to where the bald man is wrestling with the lad with the busted nose. The African spots my approach and tries to break free but Baldy has hold of his sweatshirt and I run over and have time to flick off his Real Madrid hat before I stab him three times in the face with the broken bottle.

Baldy lets go and the lad sets off running, with his friends limping behind. I turn to see Terry Cade scurry back to retrieve the holdall from under the table. He pats the bag like it's a favourite dog and grins and flashes a thumbs-up.

A crowd has gathered in the entrance of the hotel and a hotel employee is jabbering excitedly into a mobile phone.

"Lads, I think we need to get out of here before my colleagues arrive."

Baldy is rubbing at a large lump on the side of his head as he approaches and pats me on the back.

"I owe you one pal."

TC arrives with the bag shielding his face from the crowd in the doorway.

"Come on, we'll go to 'Crown round 'corner. Think we owe you a drink or two, constable."

Chapter 31

The Crown bar is five minutes' walk from the Victoria Hotel and thankfully free of any Leeds fans. We've just sat down and ordered our drinks when we hear the sirens.

Terry Cade takes a swig from his bottle and grins.

"Fuck me. Good job we swerved that. Imagine if 'Spanish law had got hold of this." He taps the bag which is positioned on the floor between his legs.

Baldy laughs and shakes his head.

"I couldn't believe it when you saw them coons scrapping with him and you were straight up, you daft old cunt."

"Old habits die hard Don. I thought I were back in 'seventies again."

Terry Cade turns to me.

"And what about you? Our Danny said you were sound but I thought...a fucking copper? " He starts laughing until that turns into a coughing fit. "You're a dark horse, aren't you?"

I shrug.

"Fucking copper on duty, bottling two wogs, fuck me! Never seen owt like it."

"Self-defence wasn't it? Shame I'm not allowed to carry my baton here or I wouldn't have needed you two."

They both laugh, then Terry Cade leans in towards me.

"Did you use to scrap with 'blacks in 'Merrion back then? Them Walsh brothers, couple of nasty fuckers them two."

I nod. "Lenton and Robbie. Yeah, I once got battered by them after the Gemini disco."

"You were a copper in London after that, Danny said?"

They're both looking at me and it's starting to feel like an interview.

"Yeah, when I came out of the army. Standard plod stuff, moved about a bit."

"How did you end up getting this job then?" Don seems to be taking a bit too much interest in my career for my liking.

"Saw it advertised in 'The Job', the copper's paper. Came up for an interview and didn't hide the fact that I was involved a bit as a kid. They seemed to like that, so I got the job."

"Involved as a kid. You're still involved now from what I hear. Mate of Shivers and them aren't you?"

"Yeah, we help each other out." I wink and take a swig from my bottle.

"You used to sell 'papers then?"

"Yeah, a bit." I don't look at Don and hope he doesn't start going into any detail on how it all worked, trying to catch me out, but I'm saved by a buzz from the Nokia in my pocket.

A Spanish number appears on the screen and I stand up.

"Better take this."

"Are you staying for another or getting off?" Terry Cade lifts his half empty bottle.

I cup my hand over the phone's microphone and hold it at arm's length.

"Why not...Get 'em in mate."

I walk to the edge of the road and look up and down, seeing an intermittent blue flash bouncing off one of the high rises round the corner.

"Charlie...Charlie are you there?"

"Hi Lorenzo, yes I'm here. Everything okay?"

"Yes, but a few incidents. Where are you?"

"I'm with an informant. He's travelled with our main lads. He thinks there's potentially going to be an attack on the police outside the stadium if Leeds lose tomorrow."

"Okay...okay. Where are you? Should I come?"

"No mate, that will spook him. I'm trying to get the details out of him. Who's involved, where they're staying tomorrow, that kind of thing."

"Okay Charlie. I'm at a hotel in Centro, there's been a fight between some Leeds fans and Africans. There's a lot of blood. Knives we think."

"Shit. Who's been stabbed?"

"Not Leeds fans I don't think. They'd all gone when we got here but the hotel staff think it was an African who was bleeding."

I turn and give a thumbs up to TC as he returns from the bar with a tray of bottles and shot glasses.

"Have you checked the hospitals?"

"Yes, but they won't go there, they'll have no papers."

"Okay. Anything else happening?"

He's laughing now. "The usual, singing, pissing in the street. Nothing we don't see every night on the strip."

"Okay Lorenzo, well, hopefully I'll get this lad talking and we can catch up later."

I kill the call then flick through the address book until I find Tony Hudson. No fucking surprise, no answer. I call Eddie Young. He answers straight away.

"How's it going there?"

He sounds well pissed off. "Nowt. A few Leeds drinking round town but fuck all of theirs. Waste of time. Owt happening there?"

"Yeah, loads of lads here. Already scrapping with the Lookie-lookies. Couple of stabbings."

"Fuck off! You're fucking lying!"

"No, it's kicking off all over. Just let Hudson know, will you? He's not answering."

"I've not seen him since we checked in. Said he had a meeting with the Jefe Comisario."

"Yeah, I can guess. Two hundred euro restaurant bill on expenses. Right, need to go, we're shorthanded here. See you tomorrow."

He starts speaking as I kill the call and head back to the table, where Terry Cade and Don have already downed their shots and are thrusting one towards me.

"Come on Charlie, have a proper drink with us. To old times, fallen comrades, Her Majesty the Queen, and England!"

I lift my glass. "You're forgetting something...to Leeds United, Champions of Europe at last!"

Chapter 32

After four more rounds of beer and shots, I've persuaded Terry and Don that it might be wise to take the bag back to their hotel, so Don and I are now sitting in a taxi in the car park, and I'm explaining that I can't go drinking round town without being spotted by Leeds fans or the Spanish police. Don is flicking through his phone's address book.

"I know just the place. Our mate's club, it's out of town in the hills up near La Nucia. There'll be no Leeds fans in there and certainly no fucking Spanish law."

He taps on the phone's keypad and presses it to his ear as the taxi driver looks at his watch and the meter ticks up to six euros.

"Hello...Hello...Dougie, is that you? It's Don mate. You okay?...Yeah, yeah, sound... Look, we're going to have a drive up...Now...we're in a taxi in town...three of us...Sound, yeah. Listen, is that Nora on tonight?...the Estonian one...little, dark hair....yeah? Sound...look could you , er...like put her on one side for me if you know what I mean."

I catch the taxi driver's eye in the mirror and his expression tells me that he has a good grasp of English.

"Sound...thanks Dougie....and erm, you've got some of those erm...same pills? Yeah? Sound...Right, we'll be there in about half an hour."

"Sorted...now where the fuck's TC?"

The three of us all stare at the hotel's reception until the lift doors open and Terry Cade emerges at speed, rubbing at his nostrils.

"Oh fuck, he's on 'gear." Don shakes his head. "I love the lad but he gets on my fucking tits when he's coked up."

Terry Cade opens the passenger side door and gets in.

"Right. Sorted. Where we going?"

"Out of town, where Charlie won't be spotted. I've rung Dougie at Magnolia, said we're on our way."

"Fucking yes! Driver, drive on! And let's have some music on."

The driver catches my eye in the mirror again and jabs at the dashboard and the radio flicks to life. TC scans through the stations until 'Red Light Spells Danger' spills from the speakers with its incessant pounding bass and Billy Ocean's rollercoaster vocals.

"Oh yes, turn it up TC!"

Don is rocking next to me on the back seat and I have to bite my tongue to stop myself asking whether they like 'coon' music.

The song lyrics are proving ironically accurate as we stop at a traffic signal and Terry Cade produces a bag of white powder, dips a key in and shovels it up his right nostril then passes the bag and key back to Don who does likewise.

I raise a hand when Don passes it to me.

"Drugs tests. We have to do one every month." I lie, but they seem to swallow it.

We eventually arrive in the car park of what looks like a large hangar, illuminated by pink lighting, at the side of a dual carriageway on the outskirts of town. We stumble out of the taxi and are greeted with heavy handshakes by two large doormen, who wave us past the payment counter and into strobe lit blackness, where a throbbing techno beat makes my teeth rattle in my head.

A wiry little man with slicked-back hair, and a red shirt unbuttoned to chest level appears through the dry ice and throws his arms around Terry and Don. They introduce me, but I can't hear what they say over the pounding music. Dougie shakes my hand warmly anyway and says something else I can't hear. He waves us through the empty club and towards a bar which appears crowded, but the customers all turn out to be employees, in the form of ten hookers sat on high bar stools. We're handed glasses of fake champagne, and Terry orders beers and shots while Don makes a bee-line for his Estonian favourite.

I lean on the bar and Terry Cade slumps alongside me and presses his lips to my ear so that I can hear one shouted word in every four. Every few minutes he positions himself in front of me and I watch his lips mouth the words 'know what I mean?' I try to gauge from his facial expression whether I should be agreeing or shaking my head in disgust.

Dougie appears with a silver tray containing a pile of powder and an assortment of pills. He selects a capsule from the tray and pops it on Terry's tongue then roars with laughter and makes a grab for TC's balls. Terry holds up a stiff fist in triumph, then turns to me and shouts something else I can't hear, then begins to assess the talent sat at the bar. Don is being led into a backroom by the Estonian girl, and TC looks like he's getting a two-for-one offer, as a teenage Thai and an eastern European with inflated lips approach and drape themselves over him.

I don't anticipate a long wait, so pick up my own beer plus TC and Don's, and position myself in some leather armchairs in a bar area, where I watch a couple of depressed looking hookers jigging on the dancefloor with two Chinese men in suits.

I wake up half an hour later and glance at my watch. The music is still pounding and the Chinese and their whores have been joined on the dancefloor by a fat Spaniard on crutches and a plump Filipina. There's another sound competing with the music, and I turn to see Terry Cade, mobile phone held tight to one ear with his finger in the other, pacing and shouting. He removes the phone from his ear and fiddles with the volume, then shakes his head and looks around, and hurries towards a green backlit sign saying 'Servicios'.

I follow him through the door, careful to avoid letting it bang shut. There's a long corridor with two doors, and I follow the sound of Terry's raised voice to one on the right with the silhouette sign of a man crossing his legs. I slowly push open the door and peer round the corner at a bank of urinals, and now I can almost hear Terry's words coming from a closed cubicle. I edge into the black-tiled room and slowly close the door to block out the techno beats, still straining to hear the one sided conversation.

"Yeah, I'm alright Danny, I'm sound, I just couldn't hear you...

No, am I fuck. I've only had three pints...

Me and Don and your mate...

No, that copper, Charlie...

Yeah, yeah, he seems sound...

Long story... we had a right do with some coons, you wouldn't believe it...

No, no, that was safe, it's stashed in 'hotel...

Right...yeah. Yeah...

What...he's coming himself? Fuck me, when did that happen?

He's in Spain now yeah?

Fucking hell Danny...

Fuck me..."

My heart is beating hard and I can feel the hairs on the back of my neck standing on end. A door bangs in the corridor and I freeze, trying to control my breathing as Terry continues. Inhale for four, hold for six, exhale for four. Stay in control.

"Three of them...right...

You've told Shivers and that other lad they can come in too...

Yeah, I understand...

Half time... right. Course I understand. No, I'm not fucking pissed Danny, alright?

They'll go to the bar at half time and I'll just tell them they can't come back until I send a text. Just me and him, yeah?

Fucking hell, do we know why he's coming himself?

Alright...yeah, makes sense I suppose. And what do I call him? Not the Pig? El Cerdo...I wouldn't remember that anyway. Senor Garcia. Yeah, I'll remember, no problem. Senor Garcia...right.

Fucking hell Danny, I wish you were here...

No, no it's fine. Course I can. Should I hand it over as soon as they get there?

Yeah, understand, I've got it. I'll check in again tomorrow. Yeah, see you mate, see you."

I gently open the door as the sound of retching comes from the cubicle and ease it silently closed, then head back up the corridor and onto the leather seats.

Terry Cade emerges shakily from the toilets and heads to the bar, where he signals for a large Scotch which he throws straight down. I approach with my mobile phone in my hand, and he turns and scratches at his scarred cheek.

"I need to go Terry, my gaffer wants to know where I am." I lean in and shout in his ear. He nods and shouts something back about Don and a taxi. I extend my hand and he takes it and I can feel the cold moisture of his palm.

"See you around."

I wave to Dougie who is helping the crutch man off the dance floor and I head for the door. I pass the two bouncers and step out into the car park. I can see two taxis parked on the main road and poke my index fingers into my ears to try and clear the techno-induced deafness.

I'm on the bottom step when I hear the door open and turn as Terry Cade shouts my name.

He makes his way unsteadily down the steps.

"What I said to you in there..." Before I can ask which bit of the unheard conversation he's referring to, he says it and it lands like a punch in my chest.

"About Andy."

I feel my legs buckle and my hair stands on end again.

"Yeah..." I whisper.

"You won't say owt will you? I mean...it were just one of them things."

I shake my head, unable to speak.

"I mean he were your mate, so I thought you might be pissed off, you know..."

I start to say I didn't know him that well, but have to stop myself as I feel my voice cracking. Terry lowers himself slowly and sits on the third step and rubs at a splash of puke on his tan moccasin.

"I've always felt bad about it, but we had no choice. The kid had lost it, he'd have said owt to get moved, he made that clear. We couldn't risk it, we'd have all gone down for a long time, some real top boys involved, you know..."

I close my eyes and breathe slowly, forcing the words out.

"Who was it at Kirklevington again? I couldn't hear in there."

TC puts his head in his hands.

"Can't remember their names. Two young lads, they were looked after. We told them how to do it, make it look like he'd topped himself. Because of his history no one thought anything of it."

I feel my eyes prickle and intercept a tear before it can travel down my cheek. I can't breathe now and I know I'm as deep as it's possible to go. An explosion of anger moves up from my chest to my brain and my fists clench involuntarily as I look down at Terry Cade, but I find myself rooted to the spot. I close my eyes and inhale. Count to four. Six. Four. I exhale and the door opens with a bang and Don appears, shirtless and sweating.

"Fucks sake TC I thought you'd gone."

Terry Cade stands slowly and puffs out his cheeks and fixes me with an ambiguous stare.

"Cheers for tonight Charlie and sorry about your pal. At least you know though eh? You can forget about it now."

He turns and walks back up the stairs, and leaves me to drown in the car park in the deepest, darkest pool I've ever been in.

Chapter 33

"What is the address, where you're meeting your team?"

The BMW is pulling off the E15 into Valencia and it's the first time Lorenzo has spoken in twenty minutes. He'd sniffed loudly to leave me in no doubt that he could smell the booze on me when I got into the car in Benidorm. He'd then smirked as he asked if I had any information on the plan to attack the police if Leeds lost. I'd forgotten about that. 'Turned out to be bullshit' had elicited a slow shake of his head as he stared ahead out of the windscreen.

I retrieve a printed WYP memo from my jacket pocket and hold it in front of him.

'Novotel, Avenida Pío XII.'

He nods but doesn't respond. I know he's going to be telling Tony Hudson about my disappearance last night but I couldn't give a fuck. I sink lower in the passenger seat, my head pulsing with pain, a feeling of nausea bubbling in my throat, and images of Andy struggling in a borstal cell as two other kids tie a belt round his neck then hoist him up through the top rail of a bunk bed.

"Can you pull over please, I don't feel very well." I cup a hand over my mouth, but Lorenzo keeps looking ahead and puts his foot down, throwing the car hard round a left hand bend.

"We're nearly there now."

I close my eyes until the car slows and draws to a halt, then I open the door and puke noisily and painfully onto the pavement.

I hear voices close by as I'm retching and glance up to see Lorenzo shaking hands with Tony Hudson. Eddie Young and EGT Pierre are standing behind them, not even trying to hide their amusement.

I stand up and put a finger to my right nostril and expel a globule of snotty puke from the left one.

Lorenzo is looking at his feet, clearly embarrassed, and Tony Hudson stares at me with his hands on his hips, blue and white striped polo shirt buttoned at the collar, looking like a high school teacher on a geography field trip, disappointed at the behaviour of the 5th formers.

"Are you fit for duty PC Mills?" He looks me up and down as I hawk up a bullet of phlegm and expel it into the road.

"Yeah, I'm okay, think I had a bad egg for breakfast."

Eddie Young snorts with laughter and Hudson glares at him.

"Any update on the incidents in Benidorm? Do we know who was stabbed?"

"Africans we think. Nothing reported." I turn to Lorenzo for confirmation.

"Illegal migrants probably. They won't go to hospital. We had a few minor incidents. Some scuffles between street vendors and Leeds fans, a few arrests for drunkenness and criminal damage. Nothing more than we get every night in Summer."

"Are you sticking around for the day? See how we police football in England?" Tony Hudson smiles and pats Lorenzo on the arm and the Spaniard looks like he's going to start laughing too.

"Ah...thanks but no, I need to get back to Benidorm." He flashes me a look and shakes Hudson's hand and heads back towards the car without acknowledging me.

"How did it go last night then? You don't know who was involved in the stabbing incident?" Hudson turns to me and wrinkles his nose as he notices a puke spatter on my jacket.

"Yes sir, I didn't want to say in front of the Spanish officer, but it wasn't Leeds fans."

"It wasn't?"

"No sir, some of my most reliable CI's were there last night and they don't know of any of our lads getting involved with the Africans. They said it was locals. Spanish drug dealers. Apparently they're involved in some sort of feud with the lookie-lookie men. I don't think Lorenzo liked it when I told him that..."

Tony Hudson nods and smirks.

"Of course...much better for them to be able to blame it on Leeds fans, especially if knives are involved."

"Never thought of that sir." I catch Eddie Young's eye and he shakes his head in admiration at my gift for instant bullshit.

Hudson glances at his watch.

"Okay, I'm meeting the Comisario at eleven. I think the plan is that we'll head out to the airport to greet the daytrip flights."

Makes sense. Watch a load of shirt-wearing straight members get put on their buses, then go for a five hour lunch with your new Spanish mate.

"PC Young knows the rendezvous details to meet the local matchday CNP coordinator. Obviously they'll be taking the lead, so you just go where they want you to. Is that clear PC Mills?"

I've closed my eyes to stop the street spinning and nod my head.

"I said is that clear? You do what the Spanish police say, you don't go off-piste to meet your 'lads' or on any secret intelligence gathering missions. Okay?"

I'm tempted to say that I'll be quite happy spending the day in a deck chair on the beach and the night watching the match in a bar, but I open my eyes to see Tony Hudson's tiny yellow teeth a foot away, his nose twitching as he tries to get a sniff of my breath.

"Message received sir. The Spanish police are in charge. I'll do what they say."

Chapter 34

'The Spanish police are in charge. I'll do what they say.'

That plan had gone pretty well for about five hours. We'd met our contact Luis at the Distrito Marítimo police station, and spent the early part of the afternoon patrolling the seafront bars near the port where most of the Leeds fans were drinking.

Luis was early thirties, tall, tanned and ruggedly unshaven. Newly promoted, it was clear he saw a Champions League semi-final against an English team with a notorious fanbase as an opportunity to flex his gym-honed muscles, and show that he could quell any hint of trouble.

"He's fucking itching for summat to kick off." For once, Eddie Young was right on the money, and I'd bitten my tongue as Luis and his entourage eye-balled chanting youths in Strongbow shirts, tore down Leeds flags strung between palm trees and lamp-posts, and shoved lads back inside bars when they spilled a couple of feet too far onto the seafront promenade.

Then a phone call from a nervous bar owner had resulted in a crackled message over Luis's radio and he'd pointed us towards three vans parked on Passeig de Neptú.

Now we're in a sidestreet near Placa Redona in the old town, heading in the direction of distant chanting.

'Bertie Mee said to Don Revie, have you heard of the North Bank Highbury...'

As soon as we turn the corner, I know we've got problems. The street is narrow and cobbled, and the three bars within fifty metres of each other have merged into one, with about a hundred lads filling the whole road. Most are holding bottles or pint glasses, but a few are clutching supermarket carrier bags full of cans , and this seems to be the cause of complaint from one of the bar owners. I spot the Seacroft Mentals flag and another from Bramley and plenty of faces I know only too well. There aren't many 'Plod's Pals' here but plenty of hostiles, and our arrival causes those on the edge of the crowd to turn and stare in our direction.

'.....Don says no, I don't think so but I've heard of the Gelderd Aggro.'

The volume of the chant fades as Luis leads his men into the street and I notice a couple of officers withdraw their batons and flick to extend them. I spot Shivers and he nods me over.

"Have you heard, fucking UEFA wankers have banned Bowyer..."

"What for?"

"Stamp on one of their players in 'home game, but they've just decided to announce it today. Corrupt fuckers. All 'team have shaved their heads. Think its to support him, like the Manson family . Don't think they've gone for the forehead swastikas though."

He's laughing and slurring and swaying as I watch a lad in a blue Munsingwear polo shirt clamber onto a chair and launch into a drunken rendition of 'Barry Prudom is our friend, he kills coppers.' Luis and his men have no idea what's being sung but the lad makes the mistake of pointing two fingers at the head of one of the officers as he begins the second verse of 'shoots the bastards one by one.' You don't need too much of a grasp of the English language to interpret the meaning, and he's hauled from the chair and spread-eagled across the table, taking a dozen pints with him as he goes down.

There's a bit of jostling and shoving and some beer is sprayed across the officers. Then a bottle is flung from the bar across the street and smashes on the far wall and I see the excitement flash across Luis's face. The Spanish police have batons drawn and are pushing the Leeds fans back as they manhandle the lad from the table. I turn to Shivers who is watching with a big pissed-up grin on his face.

"I hear you're in a box then?"

"Yeah. You know Dave the Jackal?"

"The film?"

"No, Dave, with the big pointy front teeth, from Gipton. He fixed Danny's car and he's a big lad, quite handy, so Danny said he could come in with us."

I shake my head.

"Where in the ground is the box?"

"Fuck knows. Them Mexicans are in with us you know? I spoke to TC this morning. He said their main man is coming. We're under strict orders not to get pissed." He raises a bottle of Estrella and winks.

"Show me your ticket." Eddie Young is attempting to calm the Spanish police and is looking over his shoulder, trying to find me.

"Come on Shivers, hurry up."

He produces his wallet and opens it and I snatch the folded ticket and open it and squint at the white ticket with a UEFA logo header. 'Entrada Avenida de Suecia, Puertas 3, Suite 2.'

"Watch yourself, these coppers are cunts. If you don't want to get lifted before the match I'd fuck off if I were you." I hand him the ticket back and push through the crowded street.

"Where the fuck have you been?" Young doesn't look happy, but before I can answer I'm grabbed by a lad in an Aquascutum cap who sprays beer flavoured saliva into my face.

"Have you seen that? Have you seen what they're doing to Daz? He's done nowt, they're breaking his fucking arms. Can't you stop them?"

"Back off, give me a minute!" I shove him away then force my way through the crowd towards the end of the street where the Spanish police have the lad pinned face forward against the wall.

"Luis, can we just calm it down? Let's not over react."

"They attack my men. I don't allow this." He's looking over my shoulder as he answers, and when I turn round I realise why, as Tony Hudson and a Spaniard in his sixties wearing an elaborately braided peaked cap are clambering out of a Mercedes. Luis is already prancing theatrically down the street to meet them, waving his arms and pointing back towards the bar.

"Not looking good Mills?" Tony Hudson clearly can't understand what Luis is saying to his boss, but the shaken heads and furrowed brows tell him something has kicked off.

"It's nothing. A minor incident, the Spanish have over reacted as usual."

"Well, they're in charge. We're just observing." Hudson steps aside as the Comisario produces a radio from his pocket and barks an order into it. The police are now retreating down the narrow street, ten abreast, facing the Leeds fans. They're an inviting target for more missiles, and our lads don't disappoint, with a handful of bottles and half-filled pint glasses smashing on the cobbles.

"Is okay. I call UIP. Special squad." The Comisario places a hand on Hudson's arm and Luis smiles.

"Fucking stupid." I say it loud enough for all three to hear then set off back up the street. Eddie Young is in a heated debate with Ginger Keith from York, while Pierre the photographer stands nervously to the side.

"Keith, tell your lot to get moving, they've called the riot police in."

"Ah for fucks sake, it's been fine here till you lot turned up."

"Yeah well...Spanish police." I shrug then begin moving through the crowd telling everyone to drink up and fuck off sharpish. Eddie is on my shoulder.

"You shouldn't be doing this Millsy, Hudson's watching, he won't be happy."

"Hudson can fuck off. He doesn't have to deal with the fallout if this lot get battered does he? We do..."

I hear a siren and look back down the road to see two vans pull up and begin to disgorge a squadron of robocops in full body armour and helmets, carrying riot shields and three-foot-long batons.

"Ah fuck, too late."

The lads in the street have spotted the new arrivals and most set off up the street carrying their drinks, but a hardcore of around forty aren't in the mood to retreat. I spot Harry, one of the loose-cannon twins from Lincoln. He's collecting empty bottles and trying to muster support to have a go at the Spanish riot squad, and others are putting themselves on offer, advancing down the street with arms outstretched.

"If you hate Leeds United have a go..." begins to echo across the cobbles and a couple of bottles are hurled from the back of the dwindling mob of lads outside the bar.

Eddie Young has scurried back down the street so he's behind the advancing ranks of robocops, and Pierre is stood on a bar table, camera trained on the Leeds fans, finger depressed and shooting 60 frames a second. I'm standing in the narrow street between the Leeds fans and the Spanish police, and when it becomes clear my European colleagues aren't going to stop for me, I turn towards the Leeds fans and shout.

"Fucking run lads, run!"

A couple launch their bottles before turning and fleeing but Harry from Lincoln and a handful of others are on a suicide mission and charge forward. Harry's brother Paul hurls a bar stool then disappears as a tide of black body armour engulfs him, as the riot police charge up the street in pursuit of the Leeds fans. The police are stumbling and falling over scattered chairs and tables as they try to negotiate the cobbles, and a scrimmage of bodies now marks the spot where the Lincoln twins and five others are still gamely resisting arrest. I see Luis directing his troops, while glancing over to where the Comisario and Tony Hudson are looking on approvingly.

At the top of the road the riot police have paused and are dodging occasional bottles which are being flung from the other side of the square. I pick my way along the cobbled street, crunching broken glass and stepping over upturned chairs and tables. I've almost reached the black-clad ranks of officers when a sparkle of sunlight glinting off a metallic object in the gutter catches my eye, and I stoop to pick up the Spanish police baton. I look back down the street to ensure no one is watching then quickly place it into the inside pocket of my jacket.

At the top of the road the riot police are massed, facing off with around fifty Leeds fans who are congregating across the tree lined avenue.

I push my way through them and cross the road, and am immediately surrounded by angry Leeds lads.

"Fuck was that about Charlie? No need for that...we didn't do owt!"

I don't even try to justify it.

"You know how it goes, bunch of wankers, trying to make a name for themselves. Split up and make your way down to the sea front, there's loads of Leeds down there."

"Have Valencia got any lads out?" Steve Kenny is still eager for some action.

"No, fuck all, but their coppers will make up for that. Watch yourselves, any excuse and they'll batter you or nick you or both."

I watch as the group begins to disperse and move off along Calle de St Vincent. I cross the road and smile at the riot squad who glare back at me from beneath their visors.

"You see lads, all you need to do is ask nicely and they'll move. You don't always need a big stick."

I make my way back down the cobbles to where Hudson, Eddie and Luis are waiting, and pat the inside of my jacket. You don't always need a big stick but I've a feeling this one could come in handy tonight.

Chapter 35

Beyond the lights of the city stretching into the distance, I reckon I should be able to see the sea. I peer into the darkness from the top of the corner stand where 2500 Leeds fans are located, high above the pitch of Valencia's Mestalla Stadium, and look for tell tale pin-pricks of light, ships waiting to dock or fishing boats heading out for the night. If there are any out there, they're lost in the gloom beyond the daylight glare of the floodlights, and I refocus on the pitch, far below me. The white and yellow figures are so distant it's impossible to make out any facial features or shirt numbers, so you can only identify who has the ball by their position on the pitch and the way they move.

The Leeds fans are sullen and quiet, their earlier drunken exuberance has been muted by the poor acoustics in this high corner of the ground, and the events on the pitch. After a promising start, the usual playbook for Leeds in big European games is being followed, as the Swiss referee has allowed a Valencia goal to stand even though Juan Sanchez clearly knocked the ball past Nigel Martyn with his arm.

Twenty minutes gone now and I'm getting worried. I've been scanning the crowd in the stand in front of the Corporate Suites, looking for an opportunity, but I've seen nothing. Now I screw up my eyes then raise a hand to my forehead to shield my vision from the floodlit glare.

Middle of a row in the centre of the main stand, three people standing, now four. The row in front turning round. Two rows in front turning round. Three rows in front turning round. People further along the row standing, pointing.

I nudge Luis and gesture to the binoculars hanging round the neck of the young officer with him, and he passes them over.

"Problem?"

I focus on the seats where the disturbance is taking place, but I can already see the rows in front turning back round to face the pitch, smiling and laughing.

"Leeds fans in there?"

It's looking more likely that someone has spilled hot coffee or cold beer down the back of the person in front, and in typical Spanish football fan fashion, the situation is being resolved with smiles, handshakes and napkins. From this distance though, without the aid of binoculars, it could easily be some sort of altercation.

"Yes, there's a couple of our Cat C lads in there."

"Hooligans, yes?" Luis reaches for the binoculars but I keep hold of them.

"Looks like there's only a couple of them. I know them. I'll go and have a word, persuade them to leave the stadium before it escalates." I set off down the steep steps, still holding the binoculars and ignore his shouted offer of assistance.

I see Eddie Young chatting up a female Spanish cop further down the stand, so swerve down into the concourse and drop the binoculars into a bin. I re-emerge further along, then flash my warrant card to the steward manning the gate into the main stand, making my way quickly along the gangway until I reach a staircase heading down to the lower tier. I flash my warrant card again, then again, as I pass through metal doors manned by bored looking teenagers in hi-vis jackets with lanyards round their necks.

I make my way along the concourse, occasionally climbing the steps to peer at the pitch to gauge where I am. Once I'm past the halfway line I pause and look up high to the left where the advertising hoardings are obscured by Union Jacks and St George's crosses. They're so far away I can only read the lettering on the largest flags, Maverick Whites and Tadcaster. I turn to look behind me and narrow my eyes to scrutinise the Corporate boxes.

The usual cast of characters populate the hospitality area.... Middle aged men in suits and disinterested wives and mistresses with dyed red hair and leathery skin; Rich kids in leather jackets with slicked quiffs and girls with pumped up lips and tits; Twenty-somethings in expensive suits with too-attractive partners, who are probably injured players or their agents; Two lads in Italian anoraks and jeans, standing in the seats outside the box, smoking, laughing, bottles of beer in hand. Shivers and Dave the Jackal. Behind them Don is scowling, fists clenched, urging Leeds forward. Alongside him are two muscular Hispanics in dark suits, unsmiling and with arms crossed. I can't see inside the box from my position here, so I climb the steep steps of the stand, until I'm level and around fifty metres away across a block of seats. I turn away as the play shifts, with Rio Ferdinand hoisting a clearance downfield causing the faces in the box to turn in my direction.

I feel the Nokia vibrating in my pocket and remove it to see Eddie Young's name and number illuminated on the screen. I press the red button and place it back in my pocket. With the ball back in midfield, I glance again at the box. Shivers and Dave remain standing but Don and the two Hispanics are now sitting on the backs of their seats and I can see movement inside the box behind them. Then one of the Mexicans stands up and walks to the door, pauses then enters and a strip light in the ceiling flickers to life and illuminates the room.

And there he is. Head of the Sinaloa Cartel and number two on the DEA's most wanted list. Francisco Avilés Garcia. El Cerdo, the pig. A face I've known for nearly two years sitting right next to one I haven't been able to forget for twenty.

Terry Cade is holding a large bulb of red wine in one hand and a cigar in the other. A television on the wall is showing the game with a three second delay, and TC's scarred cheek and moustache are flashed with a flickering green cast from the screen. Next to him, El Cerdo is slumped in his seat, multiple chins spilling over an unbuttoned Hawaiian shirt as he stares up at the TV. His hair is unnaturally dark for a man in his sixties, and it appears thinner than the photos I've seen of him. An intermittent reflective glint tells me that he's wearing wire rimmed spectacles that I've not seen him in before. If there's any doubt in my mind that it's definitely him, that's dispelled as he turns towards me, allowing me to see the wide, round nostrils and upturned snout which give him his nickname.

I glance at my watch - 20.29. The board goes up to show a minute of added time with Leeds pushing for an equaliser. Batty wins the ball in midfield, plays a scrappy one-two with Viduka, then knocks it into the penalty area where Alan Smith is bundled over by Pellegrino. Unsurprisingly the referee signals for a corner not a penalty, and Don stands up in the box and shakes his fist and mouths silent threats, as the Mexican heavies stand impassively alongside him. The resulting corner kick is headed clear, the half time whistle blows and the crowd around me stands, to the rattling soundtrack of fifty thousand seats being uptipped. I'm now struggling to see the corporate area but I manage to catch sight of Shivers and Dave the Jackal turning and following Don and the Mexicans into the box.

A defiant chant of 'Super Leeds' rings out from high on my left, and the Valencia fans heading down to the concourse, look up and wrinkle their noses and mutter. Leeds are still in this game and they know it.

Chapter 36

I'm on the concourse with the Valencia fans when the teams emerge for the second half, and there's the usual scramble back up the stairs towards the stand, with those still queuing for food and drink shifting impatiently and glancing at their watches. There's a large, square silver TV screen attached to the wall by a thick metal bracket, and I lean on a pillar to watch the teams take their positions as the UEFA theme tune blasts from speakers and echoes along the stand.

Valencia kick off and the half starts scrappily with neither team able to retain the ball for more than a couple of passes. Then a long ball finds Mendietta on the right wing, the blond striker floats in a cross which is headed clear by Dominic Matteo. Pablo Aimar picks up the loose ball and knocks it back to Juan Sanchez who sees a space and drives forward, then hits a speculative shot from ten yards outside the area. The ball flies beyond Martyn's outstretched arm into the left hand corner of the net.

"Fuck's sake." I mutter under my breath as the fans still on the concourse go wild, and the whole stand seems to shake around me in an explosion of noise.

The remaining Valencia fans now begin to stream past me back to their seats, all jabbering excitedly, wide smiles and rueful head shakes at having missed the goal. My phone rings again. Another missed call from Tony Hudson.

I watch the replay and remain on the concourse, which has now been virtually cleared by the early goal. A handful of die-hards remain in the queues at the bar and a couple of flustered looking supporters hurry from the toilets, still re-arranging their clothes as they barge past me.

The police officer is young, early twenties, heavy lids half closed over dark eyes, slouching in his oversized blue overalls and bulky kit. He looks up as I approach at speed and flash my warrant card.

'Policia Inglesia, con Leeds United. Vamos." I turn and beckon him to follow me and we make our way along the concourse.

He's shouting behind me in Spanish but I don't turn, just beckon him to follow me.

We reach the gents toilets and I glance both ways to see a couple of jogging stragglers heading back up to their seats, before I push open the blue wooden doors and enter. An empty row of urinals on the left faces a row of stalls on the right. The young officer is looking at me quizzically and I nod my head in response and reply in a language he doesn't understand, to encourage him to follow me to the first blue door.

I put my finger to my lips and make a 'hush' sound and point to the door. He doesn't hesitate and pushes it open and shuffles into the empty trap. He peers down the pan, then stoops to look behind the toilet bowl. He's turning to ask why the fuck I've brought him in here, as I bring the truncheon down on the side of his head with a crack. He reels backwards, eyes wide with shock and fear, grabbing hold of the toilet seat to try and stay upright, so I angle the baton half sideways and smash it hard into his forehead, knocking off his blue cap and sending him falling backwards, down onto the floor. I crouch over him, my hand feeling under the right side of his body. I locate the holster and unclip the gun.

A Heckler & Koch USP Compact. I release the magazine and check it's loaded. I put the gun down the back of my jeans, slide the bolt to lock the cubicle door, then hoist myself over the top, pausing to check the cop's eyes are closed before I drop down on the other side. There's a yellow triangle saying 'Zona en Limpieza' in the corner of the toilets so I position that outside the door and walk out onto the empty concourse.

My hands are soaked in sweat and my knees begin to tremble. The adrenaline is pumping and I can feel my heart thudding in my chest. I close my eyes and breath in through my nose for a count of four. Hold for six. Exhale for four. Repeat. Stay in control. I lean against the wall of the concourse. I feel my breathing begin to slow as I imagine the cold darkness of the water enveloping my body, the chill spreading from my feet, up my lower legs to my thighs, then onwards to my chest. Lower and deeper I sink, with the sky fading fast into the gloom above me. I open my mouth and let the cold black water fill it. I taste the filth on my tongue and drink it in, until it replaces the oxygen in my lungs. I can no longer feel the rise and fall of my chest, or hear the beat of my heart. I'm blind and alone, and the sounds and smells of the world above the surface are gone. I'm back in that familiar place, back in control. I'm so deep now that I can't breathe. Exactly where I need to be.

Chapter 37

"Hello." A man's voice. Soft Scottish accent. The line clicks, then silence, broken only by the roar of the crowd in the stand above me.

"Hello, are you there?"

The line clicks again, and I wonder if it's an answering machine, then the Scottish voice again.

"Agent Code?"

"NQ4Q"

"Handler?"

"Beekeeper."

"Sector?"

"Hexagon"

"Wait."

The line clicks twice. I push the phone harder to my right ear and place my left index finger in the other one, to cut out the stadium buzz from above.

The line clicks once.

"Charlie, is that you?" Her tone is urgent but hushed, as if I've disturbed her at the theatre or a dinner party.

"Yes. It's me. Code Blue. He's here."

"Repeat that please."

"He's here. Target A. El Cerdo."

There's a long pause and she says 'wait' and the line seems to go dead.

I shift my weight between my feet and try to calm my breathing. Inhale for a count of four. Hold for six. Exhale for four. I do that twice and I'm starting to think the call has dropped when the line clicks again.

"Where are you?" She's speaking louder now, and I guess she's extracted herself from wherever she was when she took the call.

"Valencia."

"You're in Spain?"

"Well, that's where Valencia is."

"Charlie, this is serious. Can you confirm 100% that you have eyes on Francisco Avilés Garcia and that he is presently in Valencia?"

"Affirmative."

"Okay, I need to liaise with Europol Ops Command. Stay on this line..."

"No time for that. I'm compromised. We need to move immediately to option two."

I fail to catch a muffled word and she falls silent.

"Is that a go?"

"Fucking hell Charlie..." She's whispering again, breathing hard into the mobile phone, and I imagine her pacing outside a Kensington restaurant while her husband and their friends shake their heads. 'Is she still working at that investment bank? They do work her too hard...'

"You know I can't authorise that, it'll have to go up the line..."

I was expecting that.

"There's no time for that. We have a short window in which we can deliver the objective. The choice is either option two or my legend is blown and the op is compromised. I'm not taking that risk. We've waited too long for this. I'm not standing down now."

I hear her saying shit over and over and over again with her hand over the phone.

I remove the pistol from the waistband of my jeans and feel its weight in my hand. The decision is already made so I can put a stop to the endless debate she's having with herself.

"Do you trust me?"

"Fucking hell Charlie, you can't just drop something like this on me..."

"Do you trust me? Have I ever let you down?"

"Yes, I trust you but I can't make this call..."

"You don't have to. I've made it. It's happening."

I hear her whisper Jesus, before her voice is lost to a roar from the stand above me.

"Listen Charlie, the shit is really going to hit the fan on this. We need to get you out and back here for immediate debrief. Send me a text message with the extraction location."

"No need for extraction." I slip the gun into the inside pocket of my jacket, and start walking along the concourse and up the steps towards the stand with the phone held to my right ear.

"What? You said you're compromised. How are you going to get out, get back?"

"I'm already out. I'm not coming back."

Chapter 38

I flash my warrant card at the elderly Spaniard in the smart blue suit, and he holds open the door, allowing me to leave the smoke tinged evening air of the Mestalla and enter a sterile, air conditioned corridor lined with black and white photos of past Valencia heroes. Kempes, Puchades, Suarez, Machado all stare back at me, cold-eyed and accusing from behind the glass. I reach the first door and peer through the glass panel into the box. Empty wine glasses and Estrella bottles litter the table, but most of the occupants are still downstairs enjoying the half time hospitality, with only three cigar smoking silver-hairs standing at the railing watching the action on the pitch.

I hear a roar and pause to see Batty robbed in midfield by Aimar, with Sanchez streaking forward on the right, Mendietta on the left. For a couple of seconds it's three against two, but the Argentine's first touch is poor, and Martyn collects the ball.

My feet sink into the plush blue carpet as I proceed along the strip-lit corridor and I feel like I'm walking on jelly. I pause and look at the pistol in my right hand. The gun's grip is soaked in perspiration and I can feel my heart beating hard and my knees begin to tremble. I close my eyes and breath in through my nose for a count of four. Hold for six. Exhale for four. I imagine the water, cold as ice and dark with filth, ready to consume me again. I wait for the chill, feeling it spreading from my feet and legs, up my body, slowing my heart, then flooding my brain.

I carry on along the corridor, calm again, in control, no distraction from the light of the sky anymore, only darkness surrounds me now.

Another box. Four men in a huddle, looking at some sort of promotional brochure, ignoring the action on the TV above them.

I know before I reach the next box that it's the one. I can feel it. I'm about to reach for the handle when the door opens and one of the Hispanic men in the dark suits steps out. I slip the gun behind my back and he glances at me as the door closes behind him, then turns to walk down the corridor. But he doesn't go, he pauses and turns round and looks me up and down.

"You're not mean to be back up here yet." I smile at him and he frowns.

He freezes as soon as he sees the gun and has begun to raise his hands, but has only managed to lift them to chest level when the bullet blows a gaping hole in his forehead and sends him spinning backwards, spraying blood over the thick blue carpet and the black and white photos of the Valencia heroes.

I step forward and look through the glass door. Terry Cade and Francisco Avilés Garcia are both standing, staring at me. The crack of the gun has drawn their attention from the game, and now Cade is tilting his head, his attention drawn to a spatter of blood on the glass of the door. I enter the room and Garcia quickly lunges forward towards a chair, and thrusts a hand into the pocket of a suit jacket hanging on the back. I fire the gun three times and the top of his head explodes and showers Terry Cade in blood and bone and brain.

The Pig falls to the floor, taking two chairs with him and I step forward, the gun trained on Terry Cade who back pedals, arms wide, stammering incoherently until he reaches the blood spattered wall of the box behind him.

"Charlie...what the fuck? What have you done? Do you know who that was? Fucking hell..." A large dark patch is forming in the groin area of his grey chinos and Terry Cade grabs his chest and gasps for breath as he slides down the wall.

"You're a fucking copper Charlie, what the fuck? What have you done?"

"I've done my job Terry. It's just not the job you thought I had. That bit was business, the next part is personal."

Terry Cade's eyes are wide and he gulps and gasps like a fish on a riverbank.

"Terry...Terry...take a deep breath. Inhale for a count of four. Hold for six..." I step forward, the gun levelled at his forehead. "Exhale for four....That's it. You're not dying on me yet you fucker, not until you hear why."

There's a thread of snot dribbling out of Terry Cade's nose and tears spill down his cheek.

I crouch so I'm level with him and tilt the gun so the barrel is six inches from his right eye.

"Do you remember my mate, Andy? The kid you told me about at Kirklevington?"

"What?" Terry sucks in air and exhales rapidly, slumped with his back against the wall, his face ashen and tears staining the scar on his cheek. He knows what's coming.

"That kid, my mate from school? The one you had killed? Well he wasn't my mate Terry, he was my brother. My little brother Andy."

Terry Cade shakes his head and begins to cry through his gasps, his face red, his scarred cheek flashing green in the light of the TV screen.

"No...it wasn't...it wasn't me, I lied, I had nowt to do with it. I just heard about it. I made it up."

I'm close enough now for the gun to touch the tip of his nose, close enough to smell him, smell the cheap aftershave, tobacco, red wine, the shit and piss staining his chinos.

"I'm sorry, I'm..." Terry Cade's eyes are closed when I pull the trigger but mine are open. Wide open so I can see that face, the face that has haunted me for nearly twenty years. Wide open as the bullet enters between his eyes, blowing his forehead apart, showering me in an explosion of warm blood.

I close my eyes and breath in through my nose for a count of four. Hold for six. Exhale for four. Repeat. I can't feel my heart beating, can't hear my own breathing, just the distant buzz of the crowd and the muted jabber of the commentator on the TV with its three second delay.

I pick up a napkin from the table and wipe my face, then walk to the railing, and gaze out at the floodlit green expanse as Sanchez picks up the ball on the right wing, then plays a reverse pass to put Gaizka Mendieta through on goal. Four yellow shirts are closing in, and time seems to stand still as the blond haired striker looks up for a split second, then hits the ball from just outside the penalty area. I turn away as the shot skims past the outstretched hand of Nigel Martyn into the left hand corner of the net, and the Mastella erupts again in an explosion of noise. I pick up the brown leather holdall from under the table, turn and walk towards the box door. It's over now and I'm swimming back towards the surface, back towards the light.

Chapter 39

I'm out on the street, walking fast under the main stand. On my right, the six storey apartments of Avenida La Suecia are illuminated by the flickering glow of a thousand TV screens, and cheering party-goers are spilling out onto the balconies to join the celebration.

I feel the Nokia buzzing in the pocket of my jeans. Tony Hudson's name and number flashes up on the green screen.

"Hello."

"Mills, where in God's name are you?" I smile to myself as I imagine his angry yellow teeth dancing in the white glare of the floodlights.

"Just having a walk. I wasn't feeling well."

"Not feeling well? What's wrong with you now?"

I quicken my step at the sound of a siren approaching.

"I felt like I couldn't breathe but I think I'm better now."

"Couldn't breathe? What do you mean? Since when?"

I pause.

"About 1983 I think."

"What did you say? Are you taking the fucking piss Mills?"

I spot a taxi on the corner of Calle de Micer Masco and raise my hand and wave.

"Let me assure you constable, this is the final straw. I never wanted you in the first place, and I have to say my initial concerns were well founded..."

The taxi driver slows down and indicates to stop the car as he sees me approaching.

"You're unreliable..." Actually, I'm very fucking reliable, I think to myself, but let Hudson carry on.

"You don't follow orders..." I begin to laugh quietly. I follow orders to the letter.

"You're slapdash and inefficient..." I always achieve the objective, one way or another.

"I'm pretty sure you're an alcoholic, a problem gambler too." I live my legend. It becomes me.

"And you'll never work for West Yorkshire Police again PC Mills, and that's a promise from me."

I open the door of the taxi and drop the brown leather holdall on the back seat.

"Actually Tony, I'm not a fucking PC, and I've never worked for West Yorkshire police at all."

"What did you say...?"

I push the holdall along the backseat and climb in alongside it.

"I've never worked for West Yorkshire Police pal, in fact you've been working for us for the last year."

There's a brief silence then Hudson's angry voice crackles down the line.

"I've no idea what you're talking about Mills, but I need you back in this stadium immediately. Then tomorrow..."

The taxi driver looks at me expectantly in the rear view mirror.

"Tell Eddie he can have my job Tony. I won't be needing it anymore."

The driver flicks on the indicator and prepares to pull back out onto the street.

"Aeropuerto?"

I pause then raise my index finger to tell him to wait. I can still hear Tony Hudson's voice buzzing down the line like an angry wasp as I step out of the car, end the call and drop the Nokia into a rubbish bin on the pavement.

The driver is staring at me as I get back into the car.

"What's the best hotel in Valencia?"

"Best Hotel?"

"Yes, the best, costs most money..."

The driver pauses and shrugs. "The Westin I think. Maybe can be 300 euros per night."

I sit back in the seat and close my eyes as fireworks begin to explode in the sky above the Mestalla and the people on the balconies sing and dance and wave white hankies. I glance at the holdall on the seat next to me and wipe off a long smear of Terry Cade's blood with the sleeve of my jacket.

"300 Euros? That's not a problem. Take me there please. I'm on holiday now."

Chapter 40

"Goodbye Barry, see you next week, same time. Look after yourself."

Noel Kelly watches from the door of the Hyde Park terraced house as the middle-aged man makes his way down the garden path, then turns to wave before he disappears behind the privet hedge.

Noel Kelly steps back into the hallway which serves as a small waiting room for clients who arrive early, like Barry. Always twenty minutes before his appointment. Always apologising, worried about the traffic, worried about being late, worried about being early. That's Barry.

A folded copy of the Yorkshire Evening Post lies on the seat where Barry left it, and Noel picks it up and opens the front door to see if he's returned for it, but Barry has gone.

The paper is about to be deposited into the bin in the corner of his office, when Noel Kelly spots the familiar face of his local barber on the front page. *'Flattened by the Supertram'* reads the headline. *'A church, 8 shops and a bar to make way for £487m City transport scheme.'* Noel sighs and pushes his glasses back from the tip of his nose and turns to the back page. *'Champions League Crunch Time for United'* - *'Leeds United's hopes of competing in Europe's premier tournament now rest on them beating Leicester City at Elland Road tomorrow, while hoping that Liverpool slip up in their game at Charlton.'*

Noel Kelly shakes his head and drops the paper in the bin then checks his watch. 3.15. He walks across the office and sits behind the desk with its lamp and files and its Newton's Cradle. Noel checks his desk diary - Fifteen minutes until Elaine, with her multiple relationships, her mistrust of men, her unremembered childhood traumas. Noel reaches out and takes hold of one of the silver balls on the Newton's Cradle, lifts it slowly and releases it, watching as it collides with the row of stationary spheres, propelling the ball at the other end of the row forward, then backwards again, pushing the original ball into reverse. Noel Kelly places his palms on the desk and lowers his head to rest his chin on the backs of his hands, and stares hard at the silver balls. Two scientific principles - the conservation of momentum and energy transfer. The chain reaction shows how energy and momentum are maintained, providing there's minimal friction or air resistance. Just like mental health. Too much friction, too many knock-backs and eventually most people will grind to a halt and need someone to drop that silver ball and get them moving again. Someone like him. He used to trot that clever analogy out to every patient when he first started in the job, using the relaxing click-clack rhythm of the balls as an ice breaker.

"What a load of fecking bollocks." Noel smiles.

A red light is flashing on the answer machine next to the desk phone, and Noel extends a finger and presses play, and a familiar voice echoes from the speaker over the sound of the clicking balls.

"Noel, it's Charlie Mills. I'm just ringing to apologise for missing my sessions and not letting you know. Things have been a bit hectic for the last couple of weeks, and I haven't had a phone, so...sorry.

I won't be coming to see you again, but I wanted to say thank you. Talking with you helped me see things a bit more clearly. I hadn't realised how far I'd sunk down into that dark pool we talked about. I was in so deep that I'd forgotten who I was. I can see now that I'd stopped even looking for the sky, but it was there all the time. I just needed a reason to look up, swim towards it and break the surface, and our talks helped me do that, so thank you.

So…if this was a film, that would be a good ending I suppose. The shrink saves the patient and they all live happily ever after… but I don't think that's how this one ends. As I said, you helped me to see the sky again and swim back up to the surface of that dark pool of filth, and I did that. I got back there.

I've realised though…I think that dark pool is where I really belong. As you said, it's where I'm happiest, living someone else's life, not being me. So I'm going back, back into the pool, but a different one. And this time, I think I'll be going deep, deeper than ever, where there is no sky, no light. This time, I don't think there'll be any way of coming back. Goodbye Noel, and thanks."

The answering machine clicks off and the light turns green. Noel Kelly keeps staring at the silver balls until they eventually slow and lose their momentum, and finally the impact of the first ball fails to move the one at the opposite end of the row.

Noel reaches out to lift the ball between index finger and thumb, preparing to let it swing down and collide with the row and set the whole process in motion again. Instead, he pauses and looks at his own distorted reflection in the metallic sheen of the ball, Charlie Mills words echoing in his head. 'No coming back, not this time.'

Noel Kelly slowly lowers the silver ball and gently places it back at the end of the row, back where it belongs.

Noel Kelly smiles and nods. He understands now.

"Load of fecking bollocks."

More books by Billy Morris available in all Amazon stores—

Bournemouth 90

It's April 1990 and the world is changing. Margaret Thatcher clings to power in the face of poll tax protests, prison riots and sectarian violence in Northern Ireland. The Berlin wall has fallen, South Africa's Apartheid government is crumbling and in the Middle East Saddam Hussein is flexing his muscles, while Iran is still trying to behead Salman Rushdie. In Leeds, United are closing in on a long-awaited return to the first division. Neil Yardsley is heading home after three years away and hoping to go straight. That's the plan, but Neil finds himself being drawn back into a world of football violence and finds a brother up to his neck in the drug culture of the rave scene. Dark family secrets bubble to the surface as Neil tries to help his brother dodge a gangland death sentence, while struggling to keep his own head above water in a city that no longer feels like home. The pressure is building with all roads leading to the south coast, and a final reckoning on a red-hot Bank Holiday weekend in Bournemouth that no one will ever forget.

Amazon Reviews of Bournemouth 90-

"Fast paced, unflinching read."

"Well researched, 'in the know' story."

"Earthy, Leeds-based, Guy Ritchie style underworld thriller."

"The timeline & atmosphere around the build-up and description of that weekend captures just what it was like to be there."

LS92

Two years have passed, but the events of Bournemouth 90 continue to cast a dark shadow over the lives of everyone who travelled south on that hot Bank Holiday weekend. Max Jackson is out of jail and trying to re-establish himself in a Leeds underworld being torn apart by gangland warfare. The Yardsley brothers are still paying the price for their actions, with the spectre of Alan Connolly continuing to haunt them. At Millgarth, Sergeant Andy Barton finds himself in the limelight after Bournemouth, but terrace culture is changing, and police intelligence is struggling to adapt to the new normal of the nineties. At Elland Road, a resurgent United are heading towards their first league title in eighteen years, but a disturbing, malevolent force is threatening to gatecrash the champions' victory party. Old scores are settled and new ones imagined, as the climax to the title showdown becomes a deadly quest for vengeance, forgiveness and redemption. LS92.

Amazon Reviews of LS92-

"Fast moving crime thriller which picks up the pace two years on from Bournemouth 90, and captures the changing skyline of 1992 inner city Leeds, with its unforgiving streets, dubious bars and the unique characters of its time."

"If you like crime thrillers with a touch of terrace culture you will enjoy the journey this book takes you on."

"What can you say about a book that you read cover to cover in one session? There's almost no higher praise than that."

"LS92, the sequel to Bournemouth 90 is simply gripping from start to finish."

LS65

It's Spring 1965, and young Alan Connolly is a man with a plan. Out of jail and out of Glasgow, leaving old wars behind and hoping that the voices in his head allow him to forget the past. New start, new city. Smart suit, the best scooter and the right connections. LS1 is swinging - Coffee bars and clubs, pills and protection rackets. And at Elland Road, Revie's United are chasing a league and cup double in their first season back in the top flight. It's the right place and the perfect time to build his empire and the only thing that can stop him is his own dangerous ambition and the dark memories that torment him.

Amazon Reviews of LS65-

"Morris's usual heady mix of dark gritty menace, the underworld, and football set against a convincing background of the time – a culture of coffee bars and clubs, drugs and dance halls, Mods and scooters."

"Seamlessly blending fact & fiction, Morris once again draws on his great knowledge of the Leeds story- its subculture, its streets, bars & clubs, its characters, its prejudices, but most of all its football team."

"Great read, especially for anyone who's familiar with Leeds and its streets. I devoured it and finished it within 24 hours."

"Another brilliant novel by a very talented author. It is easy reading, all-action, and very entertaining. I read it in two sittings and loved it!"

Paris 75

Spring 1975. Leeds United are closing in on the only trophy that's so far eluded them - the European Cup.

In Leeds, a gangland dispute spirals dangerously out of control and leaves Alan Connolly trying to stay one step ahead of Millgarth CID, Special Branch, the Provisional IRA, a shadowy ex-CIA operative and the demons in his own head.

Leeds United's travelling army are heading for a date with destiny on a balmy May night in Paris. Their team believe they're finally about to become champions of Europe.

Alan Connolly is just hoping he can stay alive long enough to see it happen.

Gritty Urban fiction with a terrace twist from the days when it was still grim up north.

Amazon Reviews of Paris 75-

"Morris's latest book, Paris 75, wasn't the book I expected him to write. It's far better than that."

"Really catches the mood, fashion and music from the era. Takes you back to a time that many of us grew up in."

"Billy Morris is fast becoming the 'go to' man if you want to know the Leeds story."

Birdsong on Holbeck Moor

Autumn 1918. The Great War is drawing to an end and the troops are coming home. The Leeds Pals who survived the carnage of the Somme are returning to a city in the grip of a deadly pandemic, food rationing and unemployment.
In Armley, a war hero needs one more big score to settle a crippling underworld debt, but his illicit wartime schemes are over and time is running out for Frank Holleran and his family. Wartime champions Leeds City FC find themselves in the eye of a financial storm and are struggling to remain a footballing force as the full league resumes. Sports reporter Edgar Rowley is diverted from Elland Road to track an occult animal killer, while helping his brother to overcome his battlefield demons. 1919 is set to be a momentous year, but for some in Leeds, the consequences of their past actions will mean that it's never going to be peaceful. Dark, World War 1 crime fiction from the year that the City became United.

Amazon Reviews of Birdsong on Holbeck Moor-

"Refreshingly different- dark, fast-paced, with short, snappy chapters that allow the story to flow from many different perspectives."

"Thoroughly researched and well written"

"As ever the writing is tight within this book and Morris manages to juggle the various plotlines effectively."

"There are heroes and villains in this book but not in the clichéd way you find in other crime novels."

"For those that know the Leeds story - and that we've been cursed for years...then this is where our soul begins, the first stamp of our DNA."

Printed in Great Britain
by Amazon